For Nola – Niece of
My dear friend and your
Great Uncle – Cassius
– Penny Carter

Heartstrings and Tail-Tuggers

by

Penny Porter

illustrated by

Marilu Savage

Other books by Penny Porter

Fiction

THE KEYMAKER

HOWARD'S MONSTER

Nonfiction

THE BIOGRAPHY OF EUGENE GIFFORD GRACE – "as we remember him"

GREEN EGGS AND SAM

Heartstrings and Tail-Tuggers

RAVENHAWK™ BOOKS

Heartstrings and Tail-Tuggers

Penny Porter

RAVENHAWK™ BOOKS

This book is printed on acid-free paper.

Ravenhawk™ Books

Illustrated by Marilu Savage

Library of Congress Cataloging-in-Publications Data

Porter, Penny
Heartstrings and Tail-Tuggers/by Penny Porter - 1st ed, p.cm.
"Ravenhawk™ Books"
ISBN 1-893660-10-9
I. Title
99-074744 CIP

Printed in the United States of America
0 9 8 7 6 5 4 3 2 1

DEDICATION

To my husband, Bill,
who struggled to make
"Singing Valley Ranch"
a fine place to raise
cattle, horses, and alfalfa
while I fought to convert it into
"Penny's Pet Farm"
with our children
who paved the way.

TABLE OF CONTENTS

ACKNOWLEDGEMENTS

My heart is full of thanks to
Philip B. Osborne, former
Assistant Managing Editor
of the *Reader's Digest,*
whose patience and encouragement
inspired me to keep on writing,

and

to the *Reader's Digest*
for sending my stories to the world.

INTRODUCTION

Life flies by in a heartbeat, and suddenly we realize . . . far too late . . . "Hey! We always wanted to do that, but never had the nerve."

So it was, on June 14, 1967, that we tossed away the world we had known for more than eighteen years — and with our four children and brand new baby dared to take a chance on a more meaningful life, aglow with animals wild and tame amid the endless wonders of nature.

An inner nudge that a change was in store began long before I heard the sound of Bill's footsteps, a little slower than they used to be, coming down the hospital corridor. Tall, blonde, blue eyes . . . Gosh . . . I loved this guy. And even after all those years, I still thrilled at the sight of his devilish smile and the thrum in his deep bass voice. He peeked through the door. "Is she asleep?"

I nodded, and pressed my cheek against the soft down on our new baby's little round head. "She never wakes up."

He chuckled. "Till we get her home."

A seasoned father's words, I thought. Well, he should know. After all, parents never forget the *sleepless* nights and *feed me* days that come with the package labeled *newborn*. We had four teenagers, two boys and two girls. Now Becky, our fifth child, the surprise everyone laughs about, the baby my doctor said would never be because you can't have any more, was the proof that only God knows these things for sure.

Bill kissed me and laid his jacket on the foot of my bed.

"You look tired, honey," I said. Becky was only six hours old, but I knew I was nowhere as weary as Bill. He worked six, sometimes seven, days a week at his concrete block plant in King of Prussia, Pennsylvania. Time was when he liked being his own boss and never complained about long hours. But during the last few years "intruders" seemed to have taken away the joy; changes in the world beyond his control and something else, a restlessness that was worsening, a detachment I didn't understand.

"You look funny standing there in that green hospital gown," I said.

Too tired to even tie the strings in the back, he said, "Well, I think Becky and I need a little nap." He gathered the baby in his big hands, eased himself down into the comfy leather chair by my bed and laid her close to his heart. We all three slept till visiting hours were over.

•••

Bill and I met at a bridal party not long after the end of World War II. He was best man. I was maid of honor. It would be fun and romantic to say that the day we met it was love at first sight when we walked down the aisle together. Since that's the way it *almost* was, that's what we told the children when they were small. Then, when they grew up and were old enough to understand, I told them what really happened.

A party was held at my mother and stepfather's house the night before our best friends' wedding. That's when I saw a stranger standing alone, leaning against the piano on the far side of the living room. Six feet two, scarecrow thin, he seemed to be clinging to the piano for support. Ice cubes in his glass tinkled loudly in a hand that shook like a dice player's. I walked over to welcome him.

"Hi. I'm Penny," I said, conscious of the scar that puckered the left side of his face when he smiled. "Are you okay?" I asked, knowing perfectly well he wasn't. Although the evening was cool, his forehead gleamed with perspiration that streamed into the bluest eyes I'd ever seen. Nobody had blue eyes in our family.

"I'm Bill Porter." The smile broadened into an irresistibly devastating grin as he weaved dangerously toward me. Then, looking a little sheepish, he mumbled apologetically, "I guess I need something to eat."

"There's plenty of hors d'oeuvres on the dining room table."

"No." He shook his head. "I need a sandwich . . . a big one."

I was nineteen. I knew that drunks sometimes fell down and that would be embarrassing, so I grasped his bony elbow and guided him to my stepfather's library. "Sit here on the couch a minute," I said, "and I'll bring you one." By the time I returned, he'd passed out cold. I found a blanket, covered him up, shut the door and left him there till morning.

The next morning my stepfather was delighted to discover a young stranger in his library. Being Scottish, and raised an Englishman, he had great respect for fellow drinking buddies. Assuming Bill was one of his favorite *fellows*, he was surprised when the glass of amber-toned milk he offered was declined. My stepfather and I didn't know it at the time, but Bill had just returned from four years in the army with two Purple Hearts and months as a prisoner of war.

Bill and I did walk down the aisle together that afternoon. We became friends right away and fell in love just as fast. It seemed a long wait, but two-and-a-half years later, with college degrees behind us and dreams for the future, we were married, *To love, honor and obey . . . for better, for worse,* because that's the way it was done back then.

From the beginning we loved to talk. During weekends at the beach with college friends, we sat under the boardwalk out of the sun because with my red hair, and his blond, we burned badly. Also, it was fun to be away from the gang and loud music so we could hear each other. "Someday, I'd like to have a farm," he once said.

I agreed, "Me too." My happiest childhood moments had been spent on my aunt and uncle's farm on the Hudson River. "Then why are you studying to be a mechanical engineer?"

"My dad never had a chance to go to college," he said. "It means a lot to him if I go. And since the GI Bill is paying for it, well, I'd never do anything to hurt him. He wouldn't understand me wanting to farm when engineering would hold a greater future."

Two-and-a-half years gave us plenty of time to know each other, but even after we were married, like most ex-POW wives, I could never understand why Bill wouldn't talk about the war. Other soldiers did. But my questions annoyed him, so I stopped asking. How could I know that prisoners of war had been told they were *an embarrassment to the government* and to *Go home. Don't talk about it.* And above all, *Forget it!*

Forget? Like it never happened? How could they? Soldiers they had been. They had fought, been wounded, and so many never came home. They had seen their friends shot down, die from dysentery and starve or freeze to death, leaving those who were spared to stack their frozen bodies in boxcars. Healthy young boys when they enlisted, these survivors were broken men when they returned. Nobody would understand the torment locked inside these hearts until forty years later because most of these young men found the strength and courage to return to the country they loved and pursue the American dream — *If you work hard, you can be whatever you want to be.*

But scars run deep. Bill's nightmares were frightening. Shouting, groaning, trying to get under the bed and night sweats were a part of him I never understood back then. I couldn't comfort him. Sometimes, flashing outbursts of verbal temper hurt, terrifying one minute, forgotten the next. He adored our children but he couldn't tolerate any sudden noise or shrill squeal. They learned to be quiet when their father was home. "Daddy isn't feeling well today," I'd warn.

Then there were the little things that puzzled me. He hid snacks in dresser drawers, cupboards, and in his desk. He turned water faucets off so tightly there were times I had to find a wrench to open them. He screwed jar lids back on tighter than the original vacuum-packed seal. If an airplane flew too low over his car on an open highway, he would duck, grip the steering wheel and pull off the road. And he smoked — two packs a day.

"It helps my nerves," he said. When he tried to give it up, the smile was gone. Mood swings were unbearable. I begged him to start again! "Try a pipe," I said. "At least they smell better." We didn't know, back then, how harmful smoking could be. But it was the only thing that calmed him. And nearly everybody smoked. His constant spinning of the butane lighter wheel, even when the pipe was lit, raised a permanent callus on his thumb. He jumped at the ring of the telephone, doorbell or even a gentle voice in the same room if eye contact had not been made first. Most bewildering of all was his reluctance to get close to the sons I knew he loved.

We would live two lifetimes before we learned that these painful behavior patterns were symptoms of Post Traumatic Syndrome Disorder, once known as shell shock or severe nerve damage. Not until then would we understand the reason why a man was afraid to love his sons — that when a soldier is nineteen and countless young men die in his arms during battle, in prison hospitals and in prison camps, the fear it might happen again to anything male leaves a lasting imprint: *Don't get too close. Don't start loving him. He might die!*

In spite of these difficulties we were happy. Babies came fast; Emmy, Bud and Jennifer in less than three years, then Scotty not far behind. For eighteen years we thought the family was complete. We had everything the average American family needs or wants; our own house, church, friends, and children in high school. Then along came Becky.

•••

So it happened one evening, a few weeks after Becky's birth, Bill was late from work. Since four teenage appetites don't wait, and neither does spaghetti, we decided to go ahead and eat without Dad. However, I couldn't help being a little apprehensive. Fast traffic, more union threats and the need for a guard dog at the plant added to my anxiety. And Bill was *never* late for dinner. A big guy now, a hundred pounds heavier than when I first met him, he loved to eat. Meals were not only the highlight of his day, they were on the table at exactly six-thirty in the morning and six o'clock at night. Order, and no deviation from pattern, were part of his life. We ate together, the whole family, no matter who had other plans. The kids sometimes objected, but they respected their dad. That was the American way, even though most of their friends enjoyed more lenient parents.

We had almost finished eating, a plateful saved for him, when the kitchen door opened. "Sorry I'm late." He kissed me and hugged the girls. "Well," he said, "I've got news!"

Now *this* was a switch. Often a little grumpy when he got home at night, Bill rarely had much to say until after dinner. He preferred to be left alone. Pipe clenched, smoldering, lighter spinning, he disappeared into a cloud of Middleton Cherry Blend behind his newspaper until six o'clock. I, of course, wanted us all to talk right away, but his answer to that was always, "Why try? Who can compete with TV?"

But tonight . . . *I've got news?* This was different. Somehow it filled my heart with an ominous feeling. The kids fixed their eyes on Dad. I held my breath. He was not only late, he looked happier than I'd seen him look in months. His voice wasn't hoarse as it often was from arguing with union leaders or trying to convince schools that kids *need* homework. How many times had I heard him ask teachers, "Are you being fair to a student who flunks when you push him into the next grade?" And to a principal I'd heard him say, "You've got to let a kid struggle a little. How's he ever going to learn to get along in the real world?" Then he left the church where he had been the rector's warden. "Rock bands don't belong on the altar," he shouted. But no one seemed to agree with him anymore.

Now I heard the resonant bass I hadn't heard for

years, a voice so deep my mother's sofa springs used to hum when he spoke. But it was the grin that made me suspicious. Something was up, and I braced myself for the shock of my life.

"I sold the business," he announced, "and bought a ranch in Arizona. We're moving in two weeks!"

"Daddy! How could you?" The girls dashed up to their rooms crying. Bud turned the TV back on. Scott, still young enough to believe in cowboys, gaped at his dad, and I burped the baby so hard milk poured down my back.

"Arizona?" I gasped, certain that except for a hot, dusty cow town called Tucson, only Indians and asthmatics lived there. "Where?"

"Southeastern," he replied. "Beautiful desert country near the Mexican border." He might as well have said, "Near the equator."

"And you're going to raise cows on the desert?"

"Cattle! There's a difference, you know."

"Oh?"

"Beef cattle. You don't have to milk them. I'm going to buy a herd of Hereford cattle."

Tarantulas, wildcats, mountain lions and buffalo

stampeded through my mind. My memory conjured up images of rattlesnakes on sun-scorched deserts and scorpions peeking from bleached cow-skull eye sockets. Who in their right mind would go to Arizona? Only people with tuberculosis and arthritis went there — and they never came home. I finally managed to ask what I thought was a sensible, easy, get-out-of-this-thing question. "What's there for cattle to eat?"

"Browse and love grass."

I'd never heard of browse or love grass and, not wanting to sound dumb, asked the next question of myself. *How can anything grow in a part of the country where it never rains?*

Although we both had lived on farms for brief but happy weeks in our childhoods, and Bill often had talked idly about *getting away from it all and what fun it would be to own a ranch,* I always took these pipe-dreams lightly. Such fanciful conversations are part of marriage and, like books and movies, are an escape from the everyday — something different to look forward to that would *never really happen*. Now, his sudden decision was *very* real. I was stunned.

Bill was a successful businessman. He was entrenched in Rotary and active as a church vestryman, rector's warden and township supervisor; his future looked more promising every day. *"He's the only man I've ever met who should run for President,"* a friend told me. Others agreed. They pushed him, but Bill didn't want a public life. He wanted something else: the chance to recapture the vanishing American dream that had kept him alive during war. He wanted to be *alone* with his family, away from the stress of the business world and closer to God and nature.

One summer we'd bought a cottage on the Jersey coast so the children could have fun in the sun and the waves on the beach. But did Bill really enjoy it? I can count on one hand the times he managed to get away: two weekends, perhaps, one four-day week and two Sundays in winter when all the vacationers weren't there. I remember his sitting on the deck of the house just watching the ocean and taking pictures of waves by the hour. He even acquired a boat and cruised by himself. To me he often said, *"Wouldn't it be great to live on an island somewhere? Just us?"*

I didn't answer. I couldn't.

It wasn't long before he bought a camper and spent weekends looking for land to buy in the Poconos. "The roads don't go far enough," he complained, but he ordered catalogs, anyway, on how to build a log cabin. He became a good amateur photographer and spent evenings and weekends in his darkroom developing and enlarging photographs of inaccessible, mosquito-riddled lakeside lots, while I raised the kids.

Then he took a trip with a friend who wanted to move out west. His friend decided not to, but Bill returned home with slides, snapshots and movies of "Land for Sale" at the base of cold snow-capped mountains or tucked away in the forested wilderness of the *wild, wild West*. He subscribed to Sunday newspapers from Colorado, northern California, Wyoming, Texas *and* Arizona. "The climate's a little warmer down there," he assured me. Arthritis was beginning to bother him. He pored over the "Ranches and Farms for Sale" sections and the Mexican recipes in the "Food" columns. He also began studying trends in the livestock industry and ordering books on cattle. I knew his yearning for a different way of life was growing stronger. But, I kept telling myself, he had us.

Now the house and business were gone. We were leaving for sure. It would take courage to say good-bye to old friends. No one could understand. Furthermore, besides leaving our brand new home in Haverford, shaded by oaks and tall green pines and skirted by tulip and daffodil gardens I'd planted just before Becky was born, I kept asking myself, *What about the children?* They were deeply involved in school and church activities. They enjoyed a teenager's world — movies, parties, music, skiing, swimming, the Burger King, boyfriends, girlfriends, football games. This move to Arizona wasn't just a pipe-dream or another summer adventure. This was real. It was forever. And they wouldn't be coming back.

And what about me? I worked from 8:00 A.M. till 3:00 P.M. teaching at and directing the largest preschool and kindergarten in the country. I had planned to start taking Becky with me.

In 1955, with a degree in Early Childhood Education and three toddlers of my own and pregnant again, I naturally wanted to open a preschool at our house. The school soon moved to the basement of Trinity Episcopal Church in Gulph Mills, and over the next twelve years the five-day-a-week school mushroomed, reaching its maximum enrollment of five hundred three-, four-, five- and six-year-olds. It had helped finance the construction of a two-story Sunday school building, complete with individual classrooms, spacious activity rooms and three outdoor playgrounds. Trinity Nursery and Kindergarten became *the place to send your child.*

By 1967 there were thirty of us teaching at Trinity. We all loved working with young children and the chance to use our college degrees and make a little extra money. Yet we shared an even greater challenge. We all had children of our own. How was it possible to work and be home for our own children when they got out of school? Each of us solved this in her own way. Some made arrangements for their junior high and high school kids to get off early buses and help at Trinity till closing time. The few teachers who had no children to worry about doubled up on classes the last half hour in case other teachers had to leave a little early. The thought of a child coming home to an empty house was not only unthinkable, it simply wasn't done.

My timing for starting a preschool had been perfect. The baby boom of the 50's and 60's was at its peak, and Bill and I were in rhythm with the trend. With four children under six of our own, and my rapidly expanding school, I surfed the waves of success by answering a need in a changing world. The need had a name — "another mother."

I saw nothing wrong with the concept of providing day care and fun for nearly five hundred preschoolers five days a week, but in the early 60's, mothers began phoning me from the delivery room: "I want to make sure you'll have an opening at Trinity as soon as my baby is potty trained," said a voice on the line. Or, "Why don't you start a nursery group for infants? Make it a true day-care center. I've got to have some place to put this baby."

That's when I looked at our new baby, Becky, born so many years after the others, and wondered, *How could any mother think about sending anything so precious to school only minutes after birth?* Sending children to Trinity Nursery School and Kindergarten had become a community status symbol. It was the best preschool anywhere, and the changing world I had championed for so long had never bothered me before.

Now, deep in my heart, anxiety smoldered. Haunting images of three- and four-year-olds clutching blankets or teddy bears, hot tears streaming down baby cheeks as they sobbed, "I want my mommy!" cloaked my success in doubt. Was a time really coming, I wondered, when the responsibility of raising children would no longer rest with the family? One day would the nurturing of God's most precious gift become the sole responsibility of schools, towns, cities, government, television sets and computers? *What about family? What about love?*

A cattle ranch? Arizona? Soon the reality that I was being offered an escape from my part in the dismantling of the American family wrapped itself around me like a warm blanket. I hugged little Becky, feeling oddly relieved that soon I would be living in an adobe house somewhere on the Arizona desert, among tepees, Mexican casitas, sanitariums, howling coyotes and cactus.

Saturday night bridge parties, season tickets to the Philadelphia Eagles games, vacations alone at the seashore while Bill was at work, and me with swarms of kids soon would become memories in the wake of a different way of life. I was a little scared, but the dreamer, this *one-day-a-writer*, began to look forward to clean air, campfires, steak, beans and a strumming guitar under western stars. An endless vacation? What did it matter? I was ready to go, but nothing could have prepared me for this second lifetime — *another* new baby, named Jaymee, and the bonding of family life and love with fantasies of the heart.

PENNY PORTER

Heartstrings and Tail-Tuggers

July 18, 1969

When I first saw Singing Valley Ranch, I felt an overwhelming emptiness. We were still more than thirteen miles away and my stationwagon was objecting violently to the unfamiliar dirt road when I spied the "desert oasis" of Bill's dreams. "You'll know you're getting close when you see a few cottonwood trees on the horizon." The memory of his words had spun golden threads of fantasy across my mind.

What he didn't say was that the trees would be lead grey, rising like smoke amid miles of grey scrub-mesquite, spikes of parched yucca and ocotillo, brittle century plants and thorny thistle that carpeted the blistering flats of Cochise County as far as I could see. To the red-headed easterner who had already spent half a lifetime seeking shade beneath nature's green sweet-scented trees, or gathering wildflowers, or wading barefoot through brooks and lush, green grass, our new home looked like a place that God forgot.

On those barren stretches that separated our ranch from the historic gold-mining towns of Tombstone, Gleeson and Bisbee, teepee-like ant hills, eerie mirages, and devil-winds spinning up dry river beds added an alien dimension to life, if indeed there was life. Twenty-five miles to the north, Cochise's Stronghold simmered in the dust-filled air. And, twenty-five miles to the south, a twin-chimneyed copper smelter crouched on the Mexican border like a leviathan jackrabbit, polluting a sky that failed to brighten a colorless world. And at the heart of it all, beyond the mirages, Singing Valley Ranch waited for us in shades of grey, searing heat — and infinite silence.

But children and animals make things happen.

THE TAIL OF THE LOBO

I had just finished washing the lunch dishes when the screen door slammed and Becky, now nearly three years old, rushed in, cheeks flushed with excitement. "Mama!" she cried, "come see my new doggy! I gave him water two times already. He's so thirsty!"

I sighed. Another of Becky's imaginary dogs. After our old dog died and all Becky's big brothers and sisters were off to school, our remote home, Singing Valley Ranch, had become a lonely place for such a little girl. Cattle and horses were too big to cuddle and farm machinery dangerous for a child so small. Bill and I planned to buy her a puppy, but in the meantime pretend puppies popped up everywhere.

"Please come, Mama." Becky tugged at my jeans, her brown eyes enormous, pleading. "He's crying — and he can't walk!"

"Can't walk?" Now that was a twist. All her previous make-believe dogs could do marvelous things. One balanced a ball on the end of its nose. Another dug a hole that went all the way through the earth and fell out on a star on the other side. Still another danced on a tightrope. Why suddenly a dog that couldn't walk?

"All right, honey," I said. By the time I tried to follow her, Becky had already disappeared into the mesquite where the lizards and horny toads, the only witnesses to her imaginary world, basked in the desert sun. "Where are you?" I called.

"Over here by the oak stump. Hurry, Mama!"

The ring of happiness in her small voice made me feel a little guilty. I really should have come to see this new doggy days ago — the first time she asked. Now, I parted the thorny branches and raised my hand against the glare of the Arizona sun. A numbing chill gripped me.

There she was, bare toes up, heels in the sand, and cradled in her lap was the unmistakable head of a wolf! Beyond its head rose massive black shoulders. The rest of the body lay completely hidden inside the hollow stump of a fallen oak.

"Becky," my mouth felt dry, "don't move." I stepped closer. Pale yellow eyes narrowed. Black lips tightened, exposing double sets of two-inch fangs. Suddenly the wolf trembled. Its teeth clacked and a piteous whine rose from its throat.

"It's awright, boy," Becky crooned, "don't be afraid. That's my mama, and she loves you too."

Then the unbelievable happened. As her tiny hands stroked the great shaggy head, I heard the gentle thump, thump, thumping of the wolf's tail from deep inside the stump.

What was wrong with the animal? I wondered. Why couldn't he get up? Could it be rabies? Of course! Warning signs had been posted all over Cochise County, and hadn't Becky said, "He's so thirsty?" My memory flashed back to the five skunks who last week had torn the burlap from a leaking pipe in a frenzied effort to reach water during the final agonies of rabies.

I had to get Becky away. "Honey," my throat tightened, "put-his-head-down-and-come-to-Mama. We'll go find help."

Reluctantly, Becky got up and kissed the wolf on the nose before she walked slowly into my outstretched arms.

Sad yellow eyes followed her. Then the wolf's head sank to the ground.

With Becky safe in my arms, I ran to the barns where José, one of our cowhands, was saddling up to check heifers in the north pasture. "José! Come quickly. Becky found a wolf in the oak stump near the wash. I think it has rabies!"

"I'll be there in a jiffy," he said. I hurried back to the house, anxious to get Becky home. I didn't want her to see José come out of the bunk house. I knew he'd have a gun.

Back at the house I put my tearful child down for her nap. "But I want to give my doggy his water," she cried. I kissed her and gave her some stuffed animals to play with. "Honey, let Mama and José take care of him for now."

Moments later I reached the oak stump. José was already there looking down at the beast. "It's a Mexican lobo, all right," he said, "and a big one!" The wolf whined, and then we both caught the smell of gangrene.

"Whew! It's not rabies," José said. "But he's sure hurt bad. Don't you think it's best I put him out of his misery?"

The word "yes" was on my lips, but never spoken. Becky emerged from the bushes. "Is José going to make him well, Mama?" She hauled the beast's head into her lap once more and buried her face in the coarse, dark fur. This time I wasn't the only one who heard the thumping echo of the lobo's tail.

That afternoon Bill and our veterinarian came to see the wolf. Observing the trust the animal had in our child, Doc said to me, "Suppose you let Becky and me tend to this fella together." Minutes later, as child and vet reassured the stricken beast, the hypodermic found its mark. The yellow eyes closed.

"He's asleep now," said the vet. "Give me a hand here, Bill." They hauled the massive body out of the stump. The animal must have been five-and-a-half feet long and well over 100 pounds. The hip and leg had been mutilated by bullets. Doc peeled away the rotten flesh. He dug out bone splinters, cleaned the wound and gave it a dose of penicillin. Next day he returned and inserted a metal rod, replacing the missing bone.

"Well, it looks like you've got yourselves a Mexican lobo," Doc said. "He looks to be about three years old, and they don't tame real easy. I'm amazed at the way this big fella took to your little gal. But often there's a something that goes on between children and animals that we grownups don't understand."

Becky named the wolf Ralph and carried food and water to the stump every day. Ralph's recovery was not easy. For three months he dragged his injured hindquarters by clawing the earth with his front paws. From the way he lowered his eyelids when we massaged the atrophied limbs, we knew he endured excruciating pain but not once did he ever try to bite the hands of those who cared for him.

After four months to the day, Ralph finally stood unaided. His huge frame shook as long-unused muscles were activated. Bill and I patted and praised him. But it was Becky to whom he turned for a gentle word, a kiss or a smile. He responded to these gestures of love by swinging his bushy tail like a pendulum.

As his strength grew, Ralph followed Becky all over the ranch. Together they roamed the desert pastures, the golden-haired child often stooping low, sharing with the great lame wolf whispered secrets of nature's wonders. When evening came, he would return like a silent shadow to his hollow stump that surely had become his special place.

As he wandered the ranch, Ralph never chased the cattle. However, his excessive drooling when I let my chickens run loose to eat up the grasshoppers consuming my roses prompted Bill to build a fenced-in poultry yard.

And what a watchdog he was! Feral dogs and coyotes became only memories at Singing Valley Ranch. Ralph was King.

In time, although he lived primarily in the brush, the habits of this timid creature endeared him more and more to all of us. Even though Becky placed strips of meat on the dry food in his bowl, Ralph refused to eat right away. He circled the bowl, eyed the contents and drooled. Then he would lie down and wait, feign sleep sometimes for as long as twenty minutes, until something triggered his appetite. That "something" was usually a cat.

Pretending not to notice the invader, the wolf lay motionless, eyes shut. But the instant the cat's mouth touched the food he was on top of her. Fur flew as the robber streaked to safety. Ralph, his appetite now fully piqued, devoured his meal.

His reaction to humans, other than our family, is yet another story. Strangers terrified him, but his affection and protectiveness of Becky brought him out of the desert and fields at the sight of every unknown pickup or car. Occasionally he'd approach, lips taut, exposing a nervous smile full of chattering teeth. More often he'd simply pace and finally skulk off to his tree stump, perhaps to worry alone.

Becky's first day of school was sad for Ralph. After the bus left, he refused to return to the yard. Instead, he lay by the side of the road and waited. When Becky returned, he limped and tottered in wild, joyous circles around her. This welcoming ritual persisted throughout her school years.

Although Ralph seemed happy on the ranch, he disappeared into the surrounding deserts and mountains for several weeks during the spring mating season, leaving us to worry about his safety. This was calving season, and fellow ranchers watched for the coyote, the cougar, wild dogs and, of course, the lone wolf. But Ralph was lucky.

Year after year we wondered about his mate and the pups he undoubtedly sired. "Wouldn't it be fun if we could follow him and see his babies?" Becky would say. We soon learned this was impossible, for the Mexican lobo never leaves a trail. Unlike the rabbit, badger and raccoon, he never takes the same path twice.

We also learned that the wolf returns

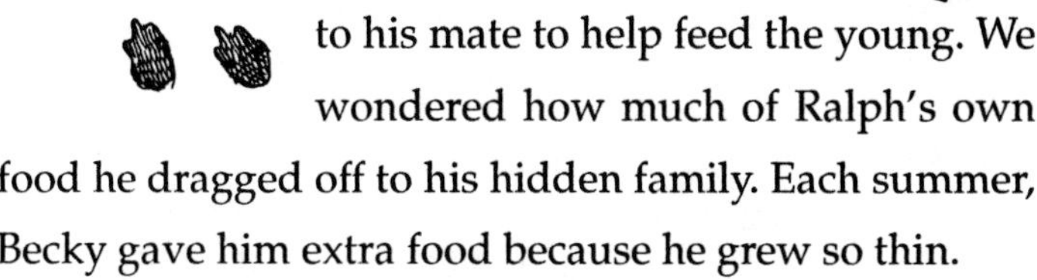

to his mate to help feed the young. We wondered how much of Ralph's own food he dragged off to his hidden family. Each summer, Becky gave him extra food because he grew so thin.

During Ralph's twelve years on our ranch, the habits of his life remained unchanged. Always keeping his distance, he tolerated other pets, endured the activities of our busy family and never wavered in his love for Becky. At last the spring came when he returned home with another bullet wound.

The next day, a rancher whose land bordered ours told us, "I got me a big she-wolf yesterday. She was runnin' with another one. I took a shot at him, too, but I guess I missed because he kept right on goin'." And came home to his family for help, I thought.

Becky was nearly fifteen years old now. She sat with Ralph's head resting on her lap. He, too, must have been about fifteen and was gray with age. As Bill removed the bullet, my memory spun back through the years. Once again I saw a chubby three-year-old stroking the head of a huge black wolf and remembered a small voice murmuring, "It's awright, boy. Don't be afraid. That's my mama, and she loves you too."

This time, the wound wasn't serious, but Ralph didn't get well. Precious pounds fell away. The once luxurious fur turned dull and dry, and his trips to the yard in search of Becky's loving companionship ceased. All day long he rested quietly.

But when night fell, old and stiff as he was, he disappeared into the desert and surrounding hills. And each morning his food was gone.

The day came when we found him dead. The yellow eyes were closed. Stretched out in front of the oak stump, he appeared but a shadow of the proud beast he once had been. A lump in my throat choked me as I watched Becky stroke his shaggy neck, tears streaming down her face. "I'll miss him so," she cried.

Then, as I covered him with a blanket, we were startled by a strange rustling sound from inside the stump. Becky looked inside. Two small yellow eyes peered back, and puppy fangs glinted in the semi-darkness. Ralph's pup! The motherless pup he had tried to care for alone.

Had a dying instinct told him his offspring would be safe here, as he had been, with those who loved him?

Hot tears spilled on baby fur as Becky gathered the trembling bundle in her arms. "It's all right, little . . . Ralphie," she murmured. "Don't be afraid. That's my mom, and she loves you too."

Did I hear a distant echo then? A gentle thump-thump-thumping of the tail of the Lobo?

September 15, 1969

At four o'clock this morning, Bill left for Reno, Nevada, with three sale bulls in the cattle trailer. He hopes to sell them at the first Golden Nugget Bull Sale sponsored by Johnny Asquaga, friend to the ranchers of the American Hereford Association.

I often feel a pang of loneliness when Bill leaves — the ranch can be such a quiet place with all the kids except little Becky off to school — but this morning after he left, I didn't feel well, and it wasn't loneliness that made my stomach turn. So, since Becky was still asleep, I put a cold breakfast on the kitchen counter for the kids and hired hands, and left a note on the refrigerator reminding Scotty to put more peroxide on his shoulder where a mother owl clawed him last night. It was his own fault. He should have left her nest alone. There were three eggs in it. Then, feeling really squemish, I crawled back into bed.

Suddenly, from a troubled sleep, I heard a chafing; then a strong scent of vinegar shocked me awake. I opened my eyes to a lobsterlike creature, at least six inches long, clinging to the inside of the window screen. Inches from my face, the vinegaroon, the largest member of the scorpion family, curled its tail over its back, let go of the screen and reached out to me. Clammy with fear and horror that any bug could be so big, I held my breath. It had eyes! What if it jumps? What if it flies? What if it stings me? I thought. No one would find me till school let out! And I'd be dead by then.

I squirmed out of bed, dashed to the kitchen, found an empty coffee can, and somehow coaxed the creature inside and slammed the lid on top.

When the monster was safe in the can, I ran to the bathroom and threw up — not because of the bug — I'm pregnant again! I know I am!

THE FLIGHT OF THE RED-TAIL

The hawk hung from the sky, as though suspended from an invisible web, its powerful wings outstretched and motionless. It was like watching a magic show — until, suddenly, the spell was shattered by a shotgun blast from the car behind us.

Startled, I lost control of my pickup. It careened wildly, sliding sideways across the gravel shoulder until we stopped inches short of a barbed wire fence. My heart hammered in my chest as a car raced past us, the steel muzzle of a gun sticking out the window. As long as I live, I shall never forget the gleeful smile on the face of the boy who'd pulled that trigger.

"Geez, Mom. That scared me!" My son Scott, fourteen, was sitting beside me. Then his face clouded. "I thought he was shooting at us! But look! He shot that hawk!"

While driving back to the ranch from Tucson along Arizona's Interstate 10, we had been marveling at a magnificent pair of red-tailed hawks swooping low over the Sonoran Desert. Cavorting and diving at breathtaking speeds over the yucca and cholla cacti, the beautiful birds mirrored each other in flight.

Suddenly, one hawk had changed its course and soared skyward where it hovered for an instant over the interstate as though challenging its mate to join in the fun. But the blast from the gun put an end to their play, converting the moment into an explosion of feathers dashed against the red and orange sunset.

Horrified, we watched the red-tail spiral earthward, jerking and spinning straight into the path of an oncoming eighteen-wheeler. Air brakes screeched. But it was too late. The truck struck the bird, hurling it onto the medial strip.

Scott and I jumped from the pickup and ran to the spot where the stricken bird lay. Because of the hawk's size, we decided it was probably a male. He was on his back, a shattered wing doubled beneath him, the powerful beak open, and round yellow eyes wide with pain and fear. The talons on his left leg had been ripped off. And, where the brilliant fan of tail feathers had once gleamed like a kite of burnished copper against the southwestern sky, only one red feather remained.

"We gotta do something, Mom," said Scott.

"Yes," I murmured. "We've got to take him home."

For once I was glad Scott was in style with the black leather jacket he loved, because when he reached for him, the terrified hawk lashed out with his one remaining weapon — a hooked beak as sharp as an ice pick. To protect himself, Scott threw the jacket over the bird, wrapped him firmly and carried him to the pickup. When I reached for the keys still hanging in the ignition, the sadness of the moment doubled. From somewhere high in the darkening sky, we heard the plaintive, high-pitched cries of the other hawk.

"What will that one do now, Mom?" Scott asked.

"I don't know," I answered softly. "I've always heard they mate for life."

At the ranch we tackled our first problem: restraining the flailing hawk without getting hurt ourselves. Wearing welding gloves, we laid him on some straw inside an orange crate and slid the slats over his back.

Once the bird was immobilized we removed splinters of bone from his shattered wing, and then tried bending the wing where the main joint had been. It would only fold half way. Through all this pain, the hawk never moved. The only sign of life was an occasional rising of the third lid over the fear-glazed eyes.

Wondering what to do next, I telephoned the Arizona-Sonora Desert Museum. When I described the plight of the red-tail, the curator was sympathetic. "I know you mean well," he said, "but euthanasia is the kindest thing."

"You mean destroy him?" I asked, leaning down and gently stroking the auburn-feathered bird secured in the wooden crate on my kitchen floor.

"He'll never fly again with a wing that badly injured," he explained, "and even if he could, he'd starve to death. Hawks need their claws as well as their beaks to tear up food. I'm really sorry."

As I hung up, I knew he was right.

"But the hawk hasn't even had a chance to fight," Scott argued.

Fight for what? I wondered. To huddle in a cage? To never fly again?

Suddenly, with the blind faith of youth, Scott made the decision for us. "Maybe, by some miracle, he'll fly again someday," he said. "Isn't it worth the try?"

So began a weeks-long vigil during which the bird never moved, ate or drank. We forced water into his beak with a hypodermic syringe, but the pathetic creature just lay there staring, unblinking, scarcely breathing. Then came the morning when the eyes of the red-tail were closed.

"Mom, he's . . . dead!" Scott pressed his fingers

beneath the matted feathers. I knew he was searching, praying for a heartbeat, and the memory of a speeding car, and a smiling boy with a gun in his hands, returned to haunt me.

"Maybe some whiskey," I said. It was a last resort, a technique we had used before to coax an animal to breathe. We pried open the beak and poured a teaspoon of the liquid down the hawk's throat. Instantly his eyes flew open and his head fell into the water bowl in the cage.

"Look at him, Mom! He's drinking!" Scott said, with tears sparkling in his eyes.

By nightfall the hawk had eaten several strips of round steak dredged in sand to ease digestion. The next day, his hands still shielded in welding gloves, Scott removed the bird from the crate and carefully wrapped his good claw around a fireplace log where he teetered and swayed until the talons locked in. As Scott let go of the bird, the good wing flexed slowly into flight position, but the other was rigid, protruding from his shoulder like a boomerang. We held our breath until the hawk stood erect.

The creature watched every move we made, but his look of fear was gone. He was going to live. Now, would he learn to trust us?

With Scott's permission, his three-year-old sister, Becky, named our visitor Hawkins. We put him in a chain-link dog run ten feet high and open at the top. There he'd be safe from bobcats, coyotes, raccoons and lobos. In one corner of the pen, we mounted a manzanita limb four inches from the ground. A prisoner of his injuries, the crippled bird perched there day and night, staring at the sky, watching, listening, waiting.

As fall slipped into winter, Hawkins began molting. Despite a diet of meat, lettuce, cheese and eggs, he lost most of his neck feathers. More fell from his breast, back, and wings, revealing scattered squares of soft down. Pretty soon he looked like an old bald-headed man huddled in a patchwork quilt.

"Maybe some vitamins will help," said Scott. "I'd hate to see him lose that one red tail feather. "He looks kinda funny as it is."

The vitamins did seem to help. A luster appeared on the wing feathers, and we imagined a glimmer on that tail feather too.

In time, Hawkins' growing trust blossomed into affection. We delighted in spoiling him with treats like bologna and beef jerky soaked in sugar water. Soon, the hawk, whose beak was powerful enough to snap the leg bone of a jack rabbit or crush the skull of a desert rat, had mastered the touch of a butterfly. Becky fed him with her bare fingers.

Hawkins loved to play games. His favorite was tug-of-war. With an old sock gripped tightly in his beak and one of us pulling on the other end, he always won, refusing to let go, even when Scott lifted him into the air and swung him around like a bola. Becky's favorite game was ring-around-a-rosy. She and I held hands and circled Hawkins' pen while his eyes followed until his head turned 180 degrees. He was actually looking at us backward!

We grew to love Hawkins. We talked to him. We stroked his satiny feathers. We had saved and tamed a wild creature. But now what? Shouldn't we return him to the sky, to the world where he belonged?

Scott must have been wondering the same thing, even as he carried his pet around on his wrist like a proud falconer. One day he raised Hawkins' perch to twenty inches, just over the bird's head. "If he has to struggle to get up on it, he might get stronger," he said.

Noticing the height difference, Hawkins assessed the change from every angle. He scolded and clacked his beak. Then he jumped — and missed, landing on the concrete, hissing pitifully. He tried again and again with the same result. Just as we thought he'd give up, he flung himself up at the limb, grabbing first with his beak, then his claw, and he pulled. At last he stood upright.

"Did you see that, Mom?" said Scott. "He was trying to use his crippled wing. Did you see?"

"No," I said. But I'd seen something else, the smile on my son's face. I knew he was still hoping for a miracle.

Each week after that, Scott raised the perch a little more, until Hawkins sat proudly at four feet. How pleased he looked — puffing himself up grandly and preening his ragged feathers. But four feet was his limit. He could jump no higher.

Spring brought warm weather and birds: doves, quail, roadrunners and cactus wrens. We thought Hawkins would enjoy all the chirping and trilling. Instead we sensed a sadness in our little hawk. He scarcely ate, ignoring invitations to play, preferring to sit with his head cocked, listening.

One morning we found him perched with his good wing extended, the crippled one quivering helplessly. All day he remained in this position, a piteous rasping cry coming from his throat. Finally we saw what was troubling him: high in the sky over his pen, another red-tail hovered.

His mate? I asked myself. *How could it be?* We were at least thirty miles from where we'd found Hawkins, far beyond a hawk's normal range. Had his mate somehow followed him here? Or through some secret of nature, far beyond our understanding, did she simply know where he was?

"What will she do when she realizes he can't fly?" Scott asked.

"I imagine she'll get discouraged and leave," I said sadly. "We'll just have to wait and see."

Our wait was brief. The next morning Hawkins was gone. A few broken feathers and bits of down littered his pen — silent clues to a desperate struggle.

Questions tormented us. How did he get out? The only possibility was that he'd simply pulled himself six feet up the fence, grasping the wire first with his beak, then his one good claw. Next he must have fallen ten feet to the ground.

How would he survive? He couldn't hunt. Clinging

to his perch and a strip of meat at the same time with one claw had proven nearly impossible. What about the coyotes and bobcats? Our crippled hawk would be easy prey. We were heartsick.

A week later, however, there was Hawkins perched on the log pile by our kitchen door. His eyes gleamed with a brightness I'd never seen before. And his beak was open! "He's hungry!" I shouted. The bird snatched a package of bologna from Scott's hand and ate greedily.

Finished, Hawkins hopped awkwardly to the ground and prepared to leave. We watched as he lunged, floated and crashed in short hops across the pasture, one wing flapping mightily, the other a useless burden. Journeying in front of him, his mate swooped back and forth, scolding and whistling her encouragement until he reached the temporary safety of a mesquite grove.

Hawkins returned to be fed throughout the spring. Then one day, instead of taking his food, he shrank back, an unfamiliar squawk coming from his throat. We talked to him softly as we used to do, but suddenly he struck out with his beak. The hawk that had trusted us for nearly a year was now afraid. I knew he was ready to return to the wild.

As the years passed, we occasionally saw a lone red-tail gliding across our pastures, and my heart would leap with hope. Had Hawkins somehow survived? And if he hadn't, was it worth the try to keep him alive as we did?

Nine years later, when Scott was twenty-three, he met an old friend in Phoenix who had lived near our ranch. "You won't believe this, Scott," he said, "but I think I saw your hawk roosting in a scrub oak down by the wash when I was home for Christmas. He was all beat up, broken wing just like Hawkins."

"You gotta go take a look, Mom."

The next day I drove north until the dirt roads became zigzagging cattle trails and finally no trails at all. When a barricade of thorny mesquite trees and wild rose bushes stopped me, it was time to walk. Finally an opening through the maze led me down to a twisting, sandy river bed: a paradise for lizards, toads, tarantulas, snakes and small rodents of the desert. It was also an ideal feeding ground for a hawk.

Flanked by the spiny overgrowth on the banks above, I walked for hours and saw no trace of

Hawkins. But hope plays such tricks on the eyes, ears and mind, I confess there were moments when the rustling of leaves, the clumps of mistletoe swaying on high branches, and the shifting shadows against gnarled tree trunks both kindled my fantasies and snuffed them out in a single second. Finding him was too much to hope for.

It was getting cold when I sensed I was being watched. Then, all of a sudden, I was looking straight into the eyes of a large female red-tail. Roosting in a mesquite less than fifteen feet away, she was perfectly camouflaged by the autumn foliage surrounding her.

Could this magnificent creature have been Hawkins' mate? I wondered. I wanted so much to believe she was, to tell Scott I had seen the bird that had cared for her mate, scavenged for his food and kept him safe. But how could I be sure?

Then I saw him.

On a low branch beneath the great dark shadow of the larger bird, hunched a tattered little hawk. When I saw the crooked wing, the proud bald head and withered claw, my eyes welled with tears. This was a magic moment: a time to reflect on the power of hope. A time to pray for the boy with a gun. A time to bless the boy who had faith.

Alone in this wild, unaltered place, I learned the

power of believing, for I had witnessed a miracle.

"Hawkins," I murmured, longing to stroke the ragged feathers, but daring only to circle around him. "Is it really you?"

Like a silent echo my answer came when the yellow eyes followed my footsteps until he was looking at me backward, and the last rays of sunlight danced on — one red feather.

May 5, 1970

Besides checking on calving cows and foaling mares during the night, my most urgent chore is to make sure the water tank never runs dry. The huge silver tank sits like an undecorated birthday cake at the top of a hill. If I see that the level is getting low, it's my job to turn a valve so it fills. But the tank — and the valve — are both on top of the hill, one hundred yards up a path of jagged, loose rocks flanked by cholla, prickly pear cactus and camouflaged rattlesnakes. The baby is due in two weeks. I'm huge, klutzy, and uncomfortable. Usually, by the time I reach the tank I'm having one of two things: a baby — or a heart attack.

Today, it was 107 degrees, and I wasn't eager to have either. I put off the water-tank journey till later. Bill came in hot and dusty after a day of putting in two new cattle guards to keep the cattle from meandering into the yard to eat my roses. Then it happened. While he was in the shower, we ran out of water. He was soapy and hollering. I got the message, ran up the hill and turned the valve. Not a sound. An airlock had formed in the pipes. For the next four hours, Bill, Bud and Scotty dug up pipes so the air would "bleed" out. No one got to bed till after midnight. I'm still not there — too busy rewashing rusty laundry and nursing smoldering thoughts. I guess I won't forget to fill the tank again. However, in retrospect, I really did feel sorry for Bill, all soaped up and no water to rinse, but I made the mistake of asking him why he didn't fill the stupid tank himself. "I hate that job," I told him. "Why do I have to do it?"

"I thought you didn't have anything else to do," he replied.

I don't feel sorry for him any more! Not one bit!

CYCLOPS IN LOVE

"Why do these cows always pick this crazy cold weather to have their calves, anyway?" Bill's deep voice betrayed anxiety more than annoyance. He turned up his sheepskin collar and jammed his hands deeper into his pockets as Scott and I hurried along beside him toward the barn. It was midnight, and the temperature at Singing Valley, our Arizona ranch, had plummeted to five below zero.

Valentine was a mountainous Holstein, now a month overdue. She was far too big, weighing nearly 3000 pounds, and we worried. Unlike our Hereford beef cattle, which calved out on the range, Valentine would give birth in a warm barn bedded with straw because she was special — a "nurse" cow that gave enough milk each year to raise not only her own calf but three or four others whose mothers either died giving birth or didn't have enough milk.

For three hours we watched the distressed animal sniffing and pawing the straw while her labor progressed.

Finally Valentine crashed to the ground, and with little help, she gave birth to a 140-pound heifer, twice the normal size, and the color of butterscotch. We hurried back to our own warm beds for what was left of the night.

Before dawn I went down to the barn to make sure the calf was up and nursing. I could hear it sucking noisily in the far corner of the stall. Eager for her hay, Valentine mooed a welcome. "Good old girl," I murmured, moving closer so I could scratch her ears. Then my foot struck something hard buried under the straw. A piercing squeal knifed the darkness.

Holding my breath, I backed away and opened the door to let in some light. I was unprepared for what lay before me — a hideous creature thrashing about. It was a black calf, twin to the beautiful heifer, but grotesquely deformed.

When it struggled to stand, I was appalled by its oversized head and the massive hump rising from its back. Its short, stubby legs were twisted and bent, and its hoofs were clubbed. It trembled.

Overwhelmed with pity, I sank to my knees and reached to touch it. The poor little calf bawled piteously and searched my fingers for milk. I closed my arms around its body and turned it slightly so I could see its face. My heart stopped. The calf had only one eye. How could nature be so brutal?

I don't know why we didn't destroy him. His "twin" was afraid of him. His mother despised him. When he tried to nurse, Valentine kicked him in the face, then gored him in the sides with her horns until he fell to the ground. But every time, though hurt and bleeding, the ugly little thing struggled to his feet and tried again. He was a survivor!

Determined to nurse, he watched his mother from distant corners of her stall and corral. He waited until she would lie down to rest; then he'd move in for his milk, clinging like a drowning sailor.

At first our four older children thought the calf was pretty gruesome looking, but feelings changed as they watched him struggle to remain alive. "Dad, he's so friendly," said Scott. "He totters up to the gate when Bud and I come with the feed, and won't quit being a pest until we scratch his head."

One afternoon, Jennifer came racing up the driveway from the school bus ahead of the others. She was a junior at Patagonia High School. "Mom!" She was breathless with excitement. "We're reading Homer's *Odyssey* in English and there's a story in it about a one-eyed giant named Cyclops! Wouldn't that be a perfect name?"

So Cyclops it was, and during the months that followed, the odd-looking calf became another ranch pet. He seemed to beg the younger children to play games with him, usually a combination of blindman's buff and hide-and-seek. They wrapped a blindfold over his eye, then ran and hid behind the tractor wheels or inside the bucket of the front-end loader. Sniffing, searching, stumbling, falling, he ran into everything, but never gave up until he found them.

Cruel? I don't think so. He was always rewarded with a hug, a lump of sugar or a pan full of sweet feed. In gratitude, he licked a hand or a small rosy cheek. "Look, Mama," a child's voice would cry. "Cyclops loves me!"

As time passed, we noticed he became a favorite of other animals wandering around the barnyard. In winter it was not unusual to find a cat curled up against the hump on his back for warmth, and in summer chickens and dogs sought shade in his shadow. We wondered if his hoofs and crooked legs were becoming painful as he grew heavier because he lay down to rest often and never without a sigh.

His best friend was Omelette, a chick we had hatched in an incubator. On their first encounter, Cyclops was napping. Omelette was less than a week old and no bigger than a bull's nostril. He began pecking at the beads of sweat running down the glistening black bovine nose. The sensation must have tickled, for Cyclops snorted loudly, blowing the chick some distance away. Undaunted, Omelette returned again and again, and finally jumped on Cyclops' face and pecked his way to where the bull's incredible horns lay.

Instead of growing up and outward, Cyclops' horns seemed to have collapsed into a tangled mound. The result was a haven for lice and horn flies, the plague of all cattle. He tried in vain to rid himself of the tortuous insects, but the snarled horns formed a perfect barrier against tree trunks and fence posts on which he scratched, desperately seeking relief.

It took only a few seconds for Omelette to discover the banquet beneath those horns. By summer's end, it was not unusual to see Omelette, now a full-grown rooster, perched on top of Cyclops' horny crown and pecking for hours at the hidden pests. At last our strange bull had found not only a companion who brought him comfort, but the friend he so desperately needed.

Still, Cyclops' own kind spurned him. During the first two years of his life, not a single cow, calf or bull would tolerate his presence.

Then came Christmas Eve. The children had just finished decorating the tree when I heard one of the girls say, "I wish the cows weren't always so mean to Cyclops."

There was a short silence. Then Scott said. "Hey you guys, I've got an idea. Let's light him up!" In seconds he was out the door with the extra strand of tree lights we hadn't needed. His sisters trooped after him. Soon squeals of laughter rang from the back pasture. I got up and opened the drapes.

Like jewels on a crown, the festive lights blinked merrily from the top of Cyclops' head. Scott had attached a small battery pack to the strand, which he had wound around the bull's horns. Curious by nature, the cows ambled up to the solitary bull one by one, and it wasn't long before he was surrounded. "They're coming to see *him*!" Becky squealed. "He thinks he has friends."

Back in the house, five-year-old Jaymee pressed her nose against the plate glass window. "And he's smiling," she said, "because they *love* him."

By the time Cyclops was three, we tried to avoid any conversation concerning how useless he was to the ranch. Bill raised pedigreed Hereford bulls. Why were we wasting time and money to keep alive this tragic mistake of nature lacking even the capacity for breeding? Cyclops had become a costly pet — he now ate nearly a ton of hay a month and had grown to weigh 1700 pounds. What possible purpose could he have?

Spring brought the breeding season. Bulls were turned out into designated pastures with cows of specific bloodlines. Except for twenty heifers that Bill planned to artificially inseminate, the rest of the herd would be pasture bred.

Heat detection is probably the most time consuming and frustrating part of artificial breeding. Hours are wasted watching for behavioral signals that would tell whether the cows were ready to be inseminated.

Cyclops was no longer free to roam. The herd bulls might consider him a threat, and cows might attack him if he ventured too close to the calves. Confined to a corral, he became frantic with loneliness. He paced. He pawed. He bawled until his squeaky voice became a whisper. Finally he stopped eating.

"He's going to die," I told Bill.

"Perhaps it's time we let nature take over," he said. But Cyclops' survival instinct prevailed and he started eating again.

Several months passed and, of twenty heifers, only

two that we could be certain of had come into heat. Bill was getting discouraged about the insemination program. Then we noticed Cyclops had stopped pacing. Instead he gazed longingly over his corral fence at a young heifer. For hours they called back and forth to one another, she in her soft alto, he in his high falsetto. "I wonder," Bill said, "if that poor thing knows something we don't?"

"Let's let him loose and find out," said Scott. "After all, he can't breed. What harm can he do?"

We opened the gate.

Cyclops, nostrils flared, snorted loudly and lurched into the pasture on those short twisted legs. At first the heifers scattered like leaves in the wind, but nothing would stop his pursuit until he found the object of his desire. He squealed. She froze. Cautiously he approached, tilting his head upward to caress her neck with his velvet mouth, her sides with his nose and chin. Finally she allowed him to rest his head against her shoulder. He could do no more. We knew then she was ready to breed. Why, I often wonder, did we not suspect sooner that fantasies beyond human understanding might be lurking in this gentle animal's heart?

For the next two years Cyclops became our "heat detecting" bull and found each cow and heifer for us as they cycled. We had a 98% conception rate that first year and 100% the second. Our homely bull was no longer lonely.

Cyclops was only four and a half years old when he died. We found him beneath his favorite shade tree where he often paused to rest and enjoy the desert breezes. His heart had simply stopped beating. As I knelt down and ran my fingers along his neck, a lump rose in my throat.

I looked at the children fighting tears too. Suddenly I realized that our extraordinary bull, with his constant need for unquestioning love, had awakened something in all of us — a greater sympathy, a deeper understanding for those less fortunate than ourselves.

Cyclops was different only on the outside. Inside he had the same feelings and passion for life cherished by all God's creatures. He loved us — and we loved him.

September 15, 1973

This morning Bill planned to spend the day spraying the cattle for horn and heel flies. When he discovered he didn't have enough spray, he asked me to run to Tucson and pick up some more. First, Jaymee and I dropped Becky off at the bus stop, a crossroads in the middle of nowhere. Since the Salcido girls, whose father manages a big pecan orchard in the valley, were already waiting there, and the oldest is thirteen, I figured Becky would be safe. Then we stopped back at the ranch to make lunch for the guys before leaving.

Suddenly, Mr. Salcido came barreling down our driveway with all the children in his pickup. Waving his arms, he said, "Es oso! Es oso! Es oso!" I thought he was saying, "It's so so!"

The five girls were rosy cheeked and wild eyed with excitement. "A bear, Mama," said Becky. "Oso's a bear. Mr. Salcido was on his way back from the gas pump in McNeal when he saw the bear coming to eat us up. So he made us all get in the truck."

Mr. Salcido told me the rest of the details in Spanish. I didn't understand a word, but I thanked him, and Becky told me later he said he was going to call the ranger to come get the bear and take it back to the mountains. There are 35 children in Becky's little school. Most are Mexican. She's starting to speak Spanish and seems to understand everything — especially "bad" words.

I know we have raccoons, bobcats, skunks and porcupines. But a bear? From this day on stories will abound in our rural community. Country folk tell wonderful tales. Even though the rangers captured the animal this afternoon and returned him to the mountains, by the end of this week everyone in the valley will have his own "bear encounter" to tell, and the bear will get bigger, its fangs longer and claws sharper with each story.

CALICO TALES

They stood on the edge of the sprawling desert, a very small girl holding a kitten with blue-tinged fur in her arms and an old rancher so tall and frail he swayed like a cypress in the gentle wind.

"Boy calicos are scarce as hen's teeth," I heard him say. "Musta been that unusual blue fur that made him a boy!"

From the glint in the old man's eyes, I could tell he was a spinner of tall tales — and children are believers because their world is still so full of magic and miracles. As an adult, though, I'd always heard there were no male calicos. A genetic flaw causes them to die at birth or, at most, live only a few hours.

But this man could weave a spell, and gradually, as he went on talking, I found myself starting to believe him. A second look at this very much alive kitten — and the joy in my child's eyes — was all I needed to start doubting established fact. Maybe boy calicos could survive. And why not? Magic and miracles flourish in the great deserts of southeastern Arizona where this man had spent a lifetime. Maybe this calico was a boy.

The child hugged the ball of fluff to her cheek and, looking up, studied the face with the wrinkles pounded in from years in the sun and wind. "I'm going to name him Blueberry, Uncle Ralph," she said, "because blue's my favorite color."

"Mine too," he answered.

From the moment Jaymee and Ralph met several days before, I'd witnessed a bonding of hearts. I was in the chicken coop that morning gathering eggs, but my rooster was so nasty that Jaymee had to stay outside by herself. As she played with a stick and a bug in the dirt, I remember thinking how small and alone she looked now that Becky had started school.

Suddenly the coughing of a distant motor announced the approach of an ancient pickup crawling down the long dirt road toward our ranch. The vehicle rolled into a barnyard pothole and rocked to a stop. "Mornin', ladies," the driver said as he pinched the brim of his sweat-stained hat. "I'm Ralph Cowan. Bill around?"

"He's in the horse barn," I said, conscious of Jaymee's arms locked suddenly around my knees, the warmth of her face pressing through my jeans.

Bill had told me about Ralph Cowan, owner of the NI Ranch which bordered ours, in southeastern Arizona. A legend in his lifetime among cattlemen of the Southwest, Ralph's spread was once so vast that it took 150 horses just to keep his ranch hands mounted. The father of three sons, he'd also found time to serve fourteen years in the state legislature, two as a representative and twelve as a senator. But that was fifty years ago. Now, except for his niece Edythe, who took care of him, a few pets, and his old horse, Dodger, Ralph was alone.

He opened the door and untangled his long legs. Then, squaring his boots on the ground, he leaned forward and smiled into the solemn little face peeking out from behind me. "I'll bet you like calico kittens," he said.

Jaymee's head bobbed.

"Well, I've got a brand-new litter at my place, and as soon as they're old enough to leave their mama, how about I bring you one?"

Jaymee looked up at me anxiously. "I hope it's a boy, Mama," she murmured.

Ralph cupped an ear. "A boy you said?"

The grip tightened. "Daddy says no more girl cats!"

Ralph's blue eyes disappeared into a mask of friendly wrinkles. "Well, you tell your Daddy if it's a boy, it's worth five hundred dollars! That's more than he can get for a good yearling bull nowadays."

"Five hundred dollars!" Jaymee's eyes widened. She knew about money. She and Becky sold eggs and spent hours at the kitchen table counting and stacking coins in piles on the red checkered cloth.

"Now, don't forget," Ralph cautioned, "a boy calico is hard to find. I've been lookin' for one . . . most of my life. But we'll see if we can't find you one." As he smiled at Jaymee, a sudden warmth tugged at my heart.

"Yep," he continued, "a blue calico is as rare as a white tarantula."

"A white tarantula?" Jaymee squeezed me harder.

"They're out there somewhere," he said. "You just gotta keep looking." I didn't think that white tarantulas existed, but who was I to break the spell that Ralph had woven?

Gripping the top of the door, Ralph hoisted his lean six-foot six-inch frame from the truck and struggled to steady himself. Afraid he might fall, I wanted to reach out and help, but right away he was heading toward the barn. To my surprise, Jaymee let go of my leg and tiptoed softly in the long shadow trailing behind him.

During the weeks that followed, Ralph visited often to "talk cattle" with Bill. Sometimes, listing like a mast on a sinking schooner, he arrived on Dodger, his legs so long he could almost wrap them around the horse's middle. But most of the time he came in his truck, and it wasn't long before we realized it wasn't Bill he really came to see.

"Where's the little gal?" he'd ask. It didn't matter that sometimes he couldn't remember her name. It was the chuckle in his eyes each time he saw her that made the difference.

Then came the day when he brought Blueberry — pink nose, buttercup eyes, frosted in silvery-blue fur. Ralph told Jaymee that Blueberry was a male, but it later dawned on me that he probably said this because he wanted it to be a male for Jaymee's sake. Since Bill didn't like cats in the house, Jaymee arranged a box for the kitten on the back porch. There he could come and go as he pleased at night, and light up her world by day.

Ralph, however, became the real flame for Jaymee.

At the first sound of his pickup, she would cry, "Uncle Ralph's coming to play!" and dash to the end of our long driveway, Blueberry flailing like a mop in her arms. When they returned in Ralph's pickup, the calico cat would be reclining on the dashboard amid rusty spurs, fence pliers, bits of wire and assorted hardware, while Ralph and Jaymee, seated among springs escaping the worn seat cover, would be making plans. Soon they were searching for secrets among fallen cottonwoods and twisted mesquites and poking sticks into forbidden lairs.

"What do you and Uncle Ralph look for?" I asked Jaymee one hot afternoon as she and Blueberry shared a dripping popsicle.

"White tarantulas." She sighed heavily. "But we can't find one anywhere."

"What does Uncle Ralph say about that?"

"He says we gotta keep looking, that's all. He says that's the only way you find things in life — by believing and looking." Her face brightened. "So we find other things."

"Really?"

"Yep. Dead baby doves all over the place." She frowned. "Lazy birds. They can't even build a nest right. Three twigs! That's all they use. Then the poor little babies fall through and get killed and the mamas and daddies cry all the time. That's why they're called mourning doves. Uncle Ralph said so."

One day she dashed into the house, eyes sparkling with excitement. "Mama!" she cried. "Chickies play songs before they hatch!"

I raised an eyebrow.

"Uncle Ralph took an egg out of the incubator and pressed it against his ear. Then he let me listen. He said it was tapping 'Yankee Doodle,' and I could hear it too!"

Later that night after the children were asleep, I asked Bill, "Can you believe all those stories Ralph tells her?"

"Can't hurt her," he said. "It's all good stuff. Better than sitting in front of the TV all day watching things she's far too young to understand."

One morning I caught the unlikely pair crouched over an anthill, heads nearly touching as though there was a conspiracy between them. Blueberry, eager to pounce on anything that moved, twitched his tail nearby. "When ants build a hill around their house," Ralph began, "it means it's going to rain."

"Does Daddy know that?" Jaymee asked loudly. She had learned to speak up because Ralph couldn't hear too well.

"Maybe not, sweetheart," he said, "but next time he goes out to bale hay, you check on the ants first. If they're buildin' a hill, tell him to wait a day." He winked at me, but Jaymee believed him.

Next to Becky, Ralph was Jaymee's best friend. But he was ill, and even at four a child can worry. "He hurts, Mama," she said. "I can tell." To Becky she confided, "Uncle Ralph's going to be an angel soon. He told me so." What will happen when he's gone? I wondered. What will she remember?

Meanwhile Jaymee absorbed his wisdom like alfalfa soaks up rain, and in subtle ways we all became victims of Ralph's stories. From Ralph, Jaymee learned to whistle "Yankee Doodle" and Becky joined in. Hours and days of the same tune trying to be whistled can be nerve-shredding. "Can't get that darn sound out of my head," Bill grumbled. "It's driving me nuts!"

Then came the migration, a yearly event that prompts hundreds of huge, black, hairy tarantulas, some the size of my hand, to cross sparsely traveled Route 666 in quest of mates. Ralph had planted the seed with Jaymee — and that's all it took. "We have to go watch!" She jumped up and down.

"Maybe there'll be a white one!"

So off we went in the pickup: Becky, Jaymee, Blueberry and I, with a three-pound coffee can to put "Whitey" in. Parked on the side of the road, we watched the phenomenon as Becky counted, ". . . 307 . . . 308 . . . 309 . . ." and Jaymee kept "almost" seeing one — while I

prayed and prayed there was no such creature, knowing in my heart that nothing would make me get out of the truck. In the Southwest, tarantulas can live to be more than seventy-five years old, and they can actually jump two feet — or more. Thankfully, I was spared.

Then the monsoon season arrived, bringing torrential storms and toads and frogs by the thousands. Puddles simmered with tadpoles — then, gradually, the water began to dry up. "The pollywogs are dying, Uncle Ralph," Jaymee said, her small voice full of sadness.

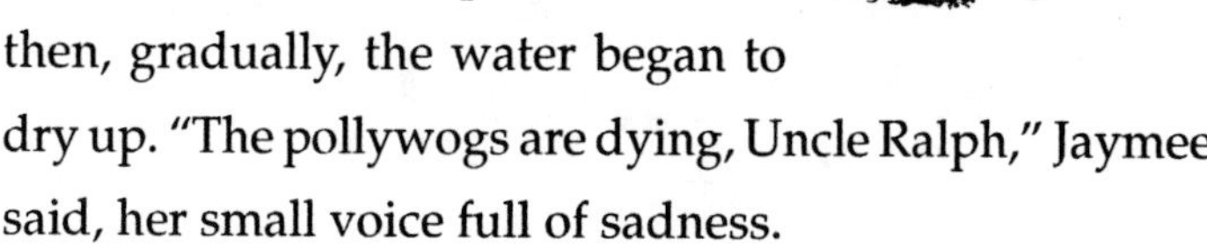

"Can't let that happen," he said. "There'd be nothing around to catch the mosquitoes — and we'd all be eaten alive!" For the rest of the day, Jaymee scurried back and forth with coffee cans full of water to keep the puddles full.

Why, I wondered, did Ralph spend so much time with Jaymee? The day she found an old box turtle living under the log pile offered a clue. "I'm going to feed him tomatoes and lettuce every day," she told Ralph.

"I'll bet he'd like Oreo cookies better." Ralph spoke slowly as he leaned down to pick up the turtle. Suddenly, he paused — then ran his stiff fingers over the worn letters carved on its ancient shell. "RC," we heard him whisper.

Of course! I thought. Ralph Cowan? Had he been the one to carve those initials years and years before? But the gentle voice of the storyteller soon rearranged my thinking.

"His name was. . . Running Coyote!" Ralph began, his eyes misting. "He was an old Indian friend of mine. He had a little girl — just like you." He looked down at Jaymee. "And he carved these initials into this shell some fifty years ago — just for her. He loved her very much."

Running Coyote? Ralph Cowan? My heart softened. Was this another tall tale? But what does it matter? I thought. The important thing was he had awakened in

Jaymee a curiosity and love for the world around her, and in her bright-eyed innocence and enthusiasm she had touched his heart and brought him back to the wonders of life. And yet, I couldn't stop thinking about those initials.

Ralph's visits suddenly stopped. A phone call from Edythe confirmed our fears. He was laid up — badly injured by a bull. "It will be a while before he can drive again," she said.

Jaymee missed him. "Can we go visit Uncle Ralph?" she asked me one day.

When we arrived at the NI Ranch, Ralph was sitting on the porch steps patting a dog so old not even a thump was left in its tail.

"Why did the bull hurt you, Uncle Ralph?" Jaymee asked.

As frail as the storyteller was, he still spun his magic. "He's old, sweetheart," Ralph said, "and his skull's getting so thick, it's squeezing his brain. It hurts. So he got mean." Jaymee nodded sadly and put Blueberry on Ralph's lap, while I went inside to talk with Edythe.

Over a steaming cup of coffee we could see the two through the kitchen window. "Wouldn't you love to hear that conversation?" I said.

Edythe smiled. "Ralph has always loved children," she said softly. "Did you know he lost his own little girl when she was about Jaymee's age? Her name was Ruth . . ."

Ruth Cowan. RC. Suddenly my mind filled with the vision of a young father scratching those initials on a box turtle for a very small girl. I pictured the two rescuing baby birds, saving pollywogs and searching for blue-calico boy kittens. And just as suddenly I knew that it was one of life's quirks of timing that had brought Ralph and Jaymee together when they were both lonely and needed a kindred spirit.

Heading home, I noticed Jaymee squeezing Blueberry much too tightly. A tiny furrow creased her forehead. "What's wrong, honey?" I asked.

"Uncle Ralph told me Blueberry's going to have . . . babies!" she said, her lip trembling. "Uncle Ralph says it's a miracle, Mama, and since only God makes miracles, to tell Daddy Blueberry's worth a lot more than five hundred dollars."

"Of course he is, honey." I hugged her close.

When Becky started school again, Jaymee didn't seem

so alone any more. She spent hours feeding cookies to RC and searching for white tarantulas. And soon she was caring for the "boy" calico's nine "miracle kittens."

The next time we visited the NI Ranch, Ralph sat huddled in an old leather chair. Edythe had arranged a wool blanket around his shoulders. Orange coils glowed from an electric heater near his feet. He smiled and talked with Jaymee and Becky. When we got up to leave, he insisted on seeing us to the door.

"Did I ever show you my cattle brand?" he asked, pointing to an empty hole in the living room ceiling. "There used to be a neon light hanging there, molded into the letters NI. His hand trembled as it covered the wall switch. "I lit it every night," he said, "a long, long time ago." His eyes sought Jaymee's. "It was blue," he murmured, "just as blue as your calico."

Jaymee stared upward at the hole, mesmerized. In her mind's eye, I could tell she saw that calico-blue light just as though it were shining down on us. And I could tell that Ralph, too, sharing Jaymee's excitement, could also see it. As ill as he was, he still loved journeying into this child's imagination.

Uncle Ralph disappeared from her life as quietly as he'd entered it, dying peacefully in his sleep. Years passed before we witnessed the absolute power of storytelling. Almost everything a small child hears and sees is tucked away in the memory. There it can hide undisturbed for years, perhaps forever, sometimes resurfacing just the way it really was — or as the heart wanted it to be.

Jaymee and Becky were in their teens, and Bill had just rewired the wagonwheel chandelier he had made for me so many years before. This time he added seven blinding-white light bulbs. "Gosh, Daddy," said Becky. "You better invest in a dimmer switch. That's so bright it's like hanging the sun in the house." She turned to Jaymee who was sitting on the floor. "Don't you think he should?"

But Jaymee's thoughts were elsewhere. Smiling, she wrapped her arms about her knees as though hugging the memory that came drifting back. "Do you remember Uncle Ralph's chandelier, Beck? The one with the NI brand on his living room ceiling?"

Becky looked puzzled. "No . . . I . . . I don't remember."

"Well, I do." Jaymee's brown eyes shone, "and when Uncle Ralph clicked the switch and turned it on, it glowed — the prettiest, warmest shade of blue I ever saw — just like my blue calico."

March 27, 1972

Last week we visited the I/V Bar cattle and horse ranch east of Douglas. George McBride, the manager, drove us out to a portion of the ranch that is now protected by the federal government. Millions of rodents have built cone-shaped, teepee-like nests that stretch for miles over the once fertile grazing land.

"Horses and cattle are breaking their legs in holes all over the ranch," he told us. "We're not allowed to shoot wild things any more, and at the rate these critters are multiplying, they're going to take over the ranch one day . . . maybe the world."

I don't really care for mice and rats too much. Emmy had a pet hamster when we lived back east. That was fine. It was in a cage. She wanted me to hold it, but I always worried it would run up my sleeve.

Mice, rats, and hamsters aren't the only rodents I've encountered. Last night I left the laundry on the line all night because the wind was so fierce I couldn't take it down. This morning, just before dawn (the only time the wind stops blowing) I finally found time to take it down. I had finished folding the sheets and was shaking out the last pillowcase when a bat, trapped inside, suddenly streaked down the front of my shirt. Trapped in my bra, it screamed. So did I. It couldn't get out! Then, wings vibrating, it tunnelled under my armpit and escaped after burrowing through my hair at the back of my neck.

I love cattle and horses and chickens, but I don't think I'll ever get used to "little critters."

A SQUIRREL FROM THE MOON

It was a quiet Arizona morning when my two little girls and I spied a baby ground squirrel beneath the thorny branches of a giant mesquite tree. The tiny creature crouched near its nest, a mound of dirt my children called "the moon." Shuffling a cactus blossom in tiny finger-like claws, it munched feversihly on a pink petal, chipping and peeping with pleasure until the eagle plunged and snatched it away from the earth. Suddenly, two more raptors that had waited above attacked the thief with their own razor-sharp talons and hooked beaks. Feathers peppered the sunrise.

That was when Becky clutched my hand and screamed. "The eagle dropped the baby squirrel — he's falling out of the sky!" Stunned, we watched the tiny creature waft to earth like and autumn leaf and land in a puff of dust.

Becky dashed to the spot where the little squirrel had landed and dropped to her knees. "Oh, Mama!" she sobbed, clasping chubby hands beneath her chin. "Do something! He's bleeding!"

When I hurried over with Jaymee in my arms, I couldn't believe it. Despite a missing tail, the baby squirrel was gadding about like a mechanical toy. Will it bite? I wondered. I put Jaymee down, cupped my hands over the terrified creature, and it curled up into a soft fur-ball no bigger than an English walnut.

I've often wondered why I didn't put the squirrel back on the moon where it belonged. Was I afraid the scent of blood would bring more predators? Or was it Becky, patched jeans and ponytails, dark eyes pleading, "Mama. He's hurt! Can't we take him home? Please? You can make him well, and I will name him 'Moonbeam'!"

I chose instead to take a deep breath of crisp April morning. Scooping the injured animal onto my palm, and telling the girls to follow, we climbed down into the wide arroyo leading to a well-worn cattle trail and home. I looked back at the top of the steep bank from where we had come, reinforcing some curious need to take with me the image of the dome-shaped mound of earth rising like the moon against a crimson sun. Pocked and abandoned, yet ringed in desert flowers, this strange phenomenon had become the heart of our magic garden, a wellspring for imagination.

From the moment we discovered it several months

ago, Becky, not yet five, and two-year-old Jaymee were certain the moon had secrets and stories to tell. They poked twigs into small round craters and peered down silent tunnels. One day Becky called, "Hello! Is anybody home?" Since no one answered, she turned to her little sister and said, "I wonder who really lives in there?"

"A man," said Jaymee, as if she'd known this all along.

"What man?"

"The man in the moon!"

Becky's dark eyes searched mine. "Does he really live there, Mama?" she asked.

Who could say no? Everyone needs a fantasy world, and soon the adventures of the man in the moon, born of love and child memory, reassured me. Kneeling in the sand, my two little girls decorated the man in the moon's house with flowers, seed pods and shiny pebbles. They sang to him and danced for him. They scolded. Blew kisses. They rolled peanuts and jellybeans down tiny passageways, and it wasn't long before the moon housed a pretend family, "just like us," Becky said, "with a mama and a daddy — and lots of little children."

Then, only a few short minutes later, the real live tenant, a round-tailed ground squirrel, popped out from the top of the moon. Like a Disney creation, the whimsical creature sat straight up on his haunches. With neck thickly ruffed and forelegs hanging over his chest, he stared at us through licorice-drop eyes — and whistled.

"A daddy squirrel!" Becky whispered, her voice a tangle of wonder and disappointment.

"Shhh!" I pressed my finger to my lips. "Watch."

From another tunnel a second squirrel appeared. Then a third and a fourth. They yawned and stretched, finally giving in to the magnetic sunshine that pulled them to the soft ground below where they thrust legs out behind them and flattened their bellies against the warm desert floor.

Soon, black eyes appeared in clusters as fuzzy babies crowded the doorways and spilled like champagne bubbles over the sides of the moon. Tails quivered in youthful anticipation, and seconds later they were tumbling and roughhousing like children penned up in the house too long before they scampered off in search of mesquite beans, seeds, twigs or succulent

cactus flowers.

Guarding four to seven babies who knew nothing of gila monsters, snakes or eagles was a full-time job for diminutive squirrel mothers, just as it was for me, a "mama" of six. Charged with anxiety, they shrilled warnings and inched repeatedly toward their own babies to bestow a "kiss" on the nose and mouth, nature's method of scent exchange aiding the tiny animals to distinguish between families, friends — and predators. But no matter how hard a mother tries to protect her young, sometimes one will roam too far. Like Moonbeam.

At dinner that night, Becky announced to the whole family that Moonbeam was a girl. Eager to show Daddy her new treasure cowering inside Jaymee's outgrown baby shoe at the bottom of a coffee can, she slid from her chair and pressed a sunburned cheek against Bill's arm. "This is Moonbeam, Daddy. Mama's going to fix up Tweetie's old bird cage for her."

"For a rodent?" Bill frowned.

"She's not a rodent!" Dark eyes sparked. "She's a squirrel!"

"Squirrels! Gophers! Mice! Rats! They're all the same.

Nothing but trouble!" He struggled to light his pipe. "They eat holes in feed sacks, gnaw leather off saddles and strip the insulation off water pipes. They even chew through electric wires!" Then he glared at me, and his eyes said the rest. "And you let her bring that thing in the house?"

When dinner was over and Bill behind his newspaper, Becky and I banked the cage with cedar shavings, filled jelly-jar lids with water, oats and cracked corn, then placed the baby squirrel, still in the shoe, inside. Becky wound up her "Brahm's Lullaby" music box and put it on top of the cage. "Now Moonbeam will have sweet dreams," she said. "That's better than nightmares about eagles."

"Yes, Honey," I agreed, "much better, and you must take good care of her until she's ready to go home."

"Home?" A small frown creased her forehead. "But I want to keep her forever."

"I know you do, " I said, "but remember — Moonbeam is a wild creature. She needs to be with other squirrels — her own family." I glanced at Bill hoping he'd heard me, but he was absorbed in the latest news affecting grazing rights on forest lands, and plunging cattle prices.

Two days passed. Moonbeam was still in the shoe. "Why won't she come out?" Becky asked.

"She's probably still scared," I said, fighting a surge of uneasiness and an unwanted thought: Maybe she's dead! I turned the shoe upsidedown and shook it. No squirrel. I shook it again and heard a scrabbling of claws. I loosened the laces and peeked inside. Moonbeam clung to the lining.

I tried to pull her out — but no tail. Nothing to grasp. I didn't want to hurt or scare her. Hadn't the eagle been enough? Gingerly, I put the shoe back, buried it under the shavings and phoned a Tucson pet store for advice. That night I told Bill that the "nice man" on the line had suggested coaxing her out with peanut butter on apple slices. "He also advised purchasing top quality hamster food with the antibiotics and vitamins a squirrel needs."

Bill nearly bit the stem off his pipe. "Antibiotics and vitamins for a rat!" I knew Moonbeam's stay wasn't going to be easy.

The little squirrel spent the rest of the week snatching morsels of peanut-buttered apple, stowing them away under the shavings, then foraging frantically to find them. "Isn't she cute?" Becky crooned. I wanted to agree, but vacuuming peanut butter shavings and apple from the rug every day was becoming a pain.

Maybe, I wondered, she'd feel more at home if we built her a moon? So we buried the baby shoe under a small bucket of earth on the bottom of the cage. And waited. Moonbeam dug her way out. Shiny black eyes appraised the situation, and while she engineered several more tunnels, Becky decorated the new moon with leaves, pebbles and wildflowers, and told her stories about snakes, coyotes and "nasty old eagles." "You're safe with me, sweetheart," she'd say.

For how long? I wondered, remembering other creatures who viewed Moonbeam with different eyes. Moonbeam's chirps, peeps and whistles brought cats by the dozen from the barns. I cannot count the times I detached would-be predators' claws from the screen door. Ever since Becky's Tweetie had fallen victim to a crafty tabby that opened unlatched doors, we hadn't dared try another bird in a cage. Now we housed something even more tantalizing: Moonbeam.

But for children, danger dissolves in the promise of mischief and fun. Home from school, dinner on the table, Daddy late, our teenagers delighted in teaching Moonbeam tricks. Jenny placed her on the lazy Susan in the middle of the table where the little squirrel played hide-and-seek among the salt and pepper shakers and vitamin bottles. Emmy helped her straddle the ceramic cow on the sugar bowl lid while Bud fed her an unwanted pea or lima bean from his plate.

One night Scott said, "Let's give her a ride!" As the Susan turned, Moonbeam trilled and peeped with surprise.

"She thinks it's a merry-go-round!" Becky clapped her hands. Encouraged, Scott gave the Susan an overly enthusiastic shove, propelling Moonbeam from her merry-go-round to the table edge. Fearing she might jump off, he quickly turned his empty water glass upside down on top of her. "Hey! Look at that!" he said as Moonbeam sat up and licked moisture off the inside of the glass. "She looks like a space creature on the *Enterprise*, transported from another planet."

"She is from the moon," I reminded him.

"Oh, Mom!" Groans chorused around the table.

Gradually, I too became smitten by the surprising intelligence reflected in Moonbeam's way-too-big, satin-black eyes. I began taking her out of the cage, talking to her, carrying her around in my jacket pocket. She loved pockets. But magic struck when, seated on my palm, this Lilliputian creature would cock her head to one side, look me straight in the eye and chirp. Irresistible. I knew she was trying to communicate, and it wasn't long before we shared a deep, tender curiosity about one another.

Soon after, I found myself wondering if I was the only one who saw her furtive glances out the window at a world beyond.

By July, Moonbeam stood five inches high. Despite the missing tail, she looked healthy, her fur a glossy cinnamon. Increasingly, it became difficult for any of us to remember this little creature as wild. Becky spent hours at the kitchen table dressing her tiny pet in Barbie outfits and giving her rides in the doll's shiny red convertible. An empty paper towel cylinder provided even more fun. Moonbeam crawled eagerly inside and rolled the tube up and down the Formica surface until she was either dizzy or had had enough.

What did it matter? Anything that can entertain two pre-school children for long periods of time is a joy to any mother. I was convinced that Moonbeam was an exception to the rodent world, a fancy I feared Bill would never share, especially after the storm.

It was August when the devil winds blasted out of Mexico. Telephone poles snapped like toothpicks. We had an emergency generator, so I didn't worry about the power loss until 7:30 p.m. rolled around and Bill came home, jaw set, flashlight on.

"What happened?" I asked. "Didn't the generator work?"

"No! Rats chewed up the battery cable." That night I hid Moonbeam in the laundry room.

It was late October when I sensed a sadness in our little squirrel, a poignant reminder that she came from a different world, one we knew nothing about. Eyes closed, chirps gone, she spent most of her time in the baby shoe buried beneath her moon. One day, I picked her up and held her close. "Don't you die on us," I whispered, and she regarded me with such melancholy I knew I had to let her go.

I phoned a wildlife specialist at the Arizona-Sonora Desert Museum to make sure I was doing the right thing. To my surprise, he said by now Moonbeam's family scent was gone. She would be a threat to the colony. Other squirrels would kill her. "Wait till spring," he said. "The males will be looking for mates by then. She might have a chance."

Again and again I'd warned Jaymee, "Never take Moonbeam out of her cage unless Mama's there. A cat might catch her and eat her up." But Jaymee was two and a half, and the morning finally came when I found the cage door open.

"I thought she was dead," Jaymee said, lip quivering, "so I squeezed her to see and she jumped out!" Moonbeam was loose, and the cats clung like bats to the sliding screen door.

Becky was heartbroken. She crawled around the house peeking under dust ruffles, appliances and bookshelves. "Here Moony, Moony," she called. We searched, listened for chirps and peeps. I yelled, "Shut the door!" a hundred times a day for fear Moonbeam would get out or a cat would get in. And Bill reminded me she was now free to chew up any wire—the toaster cord, the TV aerial, even "the wire to my electric razor!"

Hoping to lure her back to the shoe, Becky and I baited a ramp leading up to the cage door with peanut butter, red jelly beans and strips of Bill's beef jerky for which Moonbeam had developed a passion. I thought about those big eyes and reproached myself once more for bringing her home in the first place.

Two months passed. The children were in bed. Bill was putting a log on the fire and bemoaning the cost of extra hay to get the cattle through the winter. All of a sudden Becky appeared, eyes brimming with joy. "Daddy! Mama!" she cried. "I found Moonbeam in our closet sound asleep in Jaymee's old shoe!"

Becky handed the shoe to her daddy. He poked a finger inside. "Hibernating," he said. "Too bad cows don't do the same thing." But did I hear chuckling timbre in his voice? We resurrected the cage and Bill was the one who added a tiny heat bulb so Moonbeam could sleep peacefully for the rest of the winter.

March brought bright sounds and song to the Arizona desert. I placed Moonbeam's cage in front of the screen door so she could hear the winds dusting dry grasses, the scuttle of early lizards and yearning coos of dove. More alert each day, she sat quietly, twitching her whiskers, preening — listening — until one morning a sharp trill, unlike her songs from the past, told me the time had come to set her free.

At first I thought I'd take Becky and Jaymee back to the moon with me, but what if the eagles had wiped out the squirrel colony? What if snakes and other predators lived there now? It was best I go alone, but first I would ask Bill to take care of the girls.

I found him leaning heavily on the kitchen counter talking to Becky. He'd hurt his back again and, for the first time, I noticed his sideburns silvering beneath the weathered Stetson. Becky looked so small standing on a chair beside him.

"What are you up to, sweetheart?" I heard him ask her.

"Putting red jelly beans in Moonbeam's shoe," she said. "Mama's going to leave it on the moon, and red's her favorite color." Suddenly, hot tears spilled down her cheeks. "I . . . I don't want Moonbeam to go away, Daddy," she cried. "I love her."

"But she's a wild animal, honey," he said. "Mama told you that Moonbeam needs to be with other little squirrels — her own family."

"But she'll forget me!"

"Not a chance." He hugged her tenderly. "Animals never forget those who have been kind to them." He pulled the last piece of beef jerky from his plaid shirt pocket and put it in Moonbeam's shoe among the jellybeans. "There." He grinned. "Now she won't forget me either." Becky threw her arms around his neck. "Oh, Daddy!" she cried. "You love Moonbeam too, don't you?"

Without the children the moon appeared to be an empty place, a silent mound of earth where love tales lingered and wild things once had lived. Yet as I pulled the little squirrel out of my pocket and knelt on the cool sand, a warm circle of light seemed to enfold the garden, and a tryst between fantasy and reality began.

The man in the moon whistled.

Moonbeam sat up on her haunches and chirped.

The young male ground squirrel, almost regal in his thick fur ruff, bobbed up and down, tail vibrating expectantly.

I stroked Moonbeam's tiny head, cherishing this last intimate moment with a wild creature, and marveling that such a tiny, vulnerable scrap of nature could add such magic to my life. "See, he thinks you're gorgeous," I whispered. "Now, show him how lucky he is to find an angel that fell from heaven." I opened my hand and let her go.

The little male ground squirrel scrambled down from the moon, scampered up to Moonbeam, and kissed her passionately — as squirrels do — before they bounded off into a tunnel to start a family of their own.

"Just like us," Becky had said, "a family the way it ought to be, with a Mama and a Daddy . . ." I placed the baby shoe brimming with red jelly beans and beef jerky on the edge of the moon. Yes, I mused, a Daddy who can always make room in his heart for something special . . . even a little girl and her squirrel.

January 18, 1984

When Becky reached high school she spent a lot of time helping kids with math. One day she said to me, "Nobody can read! What's going to happen when they get to college?" Indeed, the boys shone on the football field and the basketball court, but I learned that many were reading at fourth grade level and below. How unfair, I thought. They're doomed to such disappointment. I offered to tutor.

It wasn't long before frustrations from teaching mounted. Compelling materials were scarce. How could I help older teens find joy and magic in reading, experience the thrill of suspense or a tug at the heart that would make them want to read when most stories at their vocabulary level were too childish?

I started to write, not fantasies now that I'm grown up, but true stories, lessons learned from moments in real life with all its ups and downs; stories about animals, family and nature as I had come to know them. The kids loved them for they became involved in happenings meaningful to them in a world they knew. I finally dared to try to get them published.

This morning I was filling the water tanks in my chicken coop with a hose when I heard the phone ring in the tack room — a fifty-yard dash. I unbolted the door, latched it behind me, and grabbed the receiver on the eleventh ring.

"Hello!" I gasped.

"Hello," said the voice on the line. "Penny Porter? This is Philip Osborne from the Reader's Digest. *We'd like to reprint your story, 'The Tail of the Lobo,' that appeared in* Arizona Magazine.*"*

"Really?" My heart stopped.

By the time I found Bill out on the west forty, started dinner cooking and picked up the girls at the bus, it was late afternoon. But I had to tell everyone my news. That's when I remembered the hose. And my chickens!

I dashed to the coop. No clucks. No squawks. No cackles. Nothing but an ominous trickle seeping from beneath the closed door. I lifted the latch. The door flew open and a four-foot tidal wave of straw, feathers, manure, chicken feed, and half-drowned chickens flooded the barnyard.

I guess I won't get any eggs this month. But Reader's Digest *bought my story!*

GREEN EGGS AND SAM

The tin roof on my newly built chicken coop shone in the desert dawn. I tiptoed inside to gather eggs from the nests. Brown. White. White. Brown. My heart sank. Where were the blue, buff, turquoise, and pale green eggs from my Araucanas hens, the new rage from Chile sweeping the chicken world? The promise of magic in my life?

On our southeastern Arizona ranch my husband, Bill, and our six children had been content raising cattle and horses. But I wanted chickens: Leghorn, Rhode Island Red, Plymouth Rock and, most of all, Araucanas.

In my dreams psychedelic eggs hovered like small bright balloons over the ketchup and mustard jars in the refrigerator. I told Bill and the kids we'd have color-coded breakfasts — blue eggs for Daddy, turquoise for Emmy, sea-foam green for Bud, pink for Becky . . . "Every day will be Easter," I trilled. What I didn't mention was that colored eggs would add a little magic to my life, too, give me something fresh to hang on to. Finally I presented the clincher to my egg-loving husband. "Chickens could bring in a little extra money."

We ordered 100 chicks. Some would be roosters.

Six months passed. Only white and brown eggs appeared. Then my sneaker nudged something on the henhouse floor.

An egg. An ugly, mud-green egg. I stooped to cup it in my palm. Where did it come from? Not from my chickens! Or was it simply a kink in the Maker's design?

"Mama! You found Sam!" Becky piped from behind me, her five-year-old voice full of absolute certainty.

"Sam?"

Holding up her much-read Dr. Seuss book, *Green Eggs and Ham,* she pointed at the scraggly chicken-creature on page seven — then at the egg. "Sam's in there!"

Bill poked his head in the door. "What's all the commotion?" he asked.

"Just look at this egg!"

"Olive drab." He chuckled. "Looks like a hand grenade."

"What if they're all this color?" I moaned.

"What's the difference? Taste is all that matters."

To him, perhaps. But where was the magic? What happened to my dream?

Without warning, the egg in my hand took on magic of its own. Warmth surged through its smooth, elliptical walls. Life? Sam? What was inside? I had to know. The only way to find out was to hatch it.

Becky thought the mystery chick might be lonesome on arrival, so I nestled two brown eggs and a white beside it in our plastic-domed incubator on the kitchen counter. For the next three weeks we turned the egg several times a day and added teaspoons of distilled water to maintain the correct humidity. On the twenty-first morning, right on schedule, we heard the "pippin" of tiny beaks. Hatching had begun.

The eggs quivered and rocked, each movement and sound a struggle signal — the unborn fighting for birth. At last the brown and white eggs burst, releasing three soggy chicks that slowly fluffed into yellow, rust and black puffs of down. Becky named them "A," "B" and "C."

The green egg stopped moving.

"Mama! Sam gave up!" Becky cried.

"No, honey. I think he's just resting."

"Uhh-uhhh! He can't get out!" Tears welled. "He's gonna die!"

I picked up the egg and pressed it to my ear. Mournful cheeps echoed inside. Was the shell too tough? I wondered. Too thick? Should I help?

I was a beginning chicken farmer, and the pros say "never intervene" because "no hatch" is often nature's way of ridding a species of the weak — the imperfect. But I had a child with dark eyes pleading, "Mama. Do something!"

Praying I was doing the right thing, I cracked the egg and picked open a tiny hole. A gold-tipped beak popped through, and a single internal shove sent half the shell reeling across the incubator. Sam was out . . . gasping, but alive — a scraggly chick with pure white eyes embedded like seed pearls in ash-gray down.

"She's blind," Bill said that evening. "You better get rid of her now before the other chicks kill her."

Get rid of her! "But, honey. They love her. Watch!" Sam snuggled between A, B and C. Unaware of one another, the four tiny peeps pecked at chick-mash. But I knew that grown chickens are cannibalistic by nature and prey on the frail and injured of their own kind. Even if Sam survived the early months, a blind chicken could never bluff her way past the wary eyes and knifelike beaks of full-grown hens in a free-roaming flock of 100. If only I hadn't tried to help.

But on day three, Sam cuddled up in my hand, her tiny heart rapping peacefully against my palm instead of racing in terror-beats like the other chicks'. There she dozed, unafraid, like all small creatures beneath a mother's wing.

On day four I placed her on the kitchen table about twelve inches from a soda-bottle cap full of mash. Can she find it by herself? I wondered. In moments the little blind peep scuttled toward it and pecked up nearly every morsel. Satisfied, she explored the checkered tablecloth and pulled the nubby knots. When she discovered they wouldn't come loose she returned to finish her food.

Maybe, just maybe, Sam could live a life of her own. If so, she had the right to live it as best she could. Since I was responsible for that life, I had to keep her safe.

"Mama! Sam comes when I call her," Becky said one morning. "Watch!" She and her three-year-old sister, Jaymee, were sitting on the porch rug, Sam between them peeping forlornly one minute at being left alone, the next listening with rapt attention for, "Here chick, chick, chick." Then, flapping stubby yellow-tipped wings, the ball of gray fluff darted back and forth between child voices, touching, exploring and pecking softly at little mash-filled hands. When the excitement ended, she crouched unmoving, as though trapped within invisible boundaries she dared not roam beyond.

As Sam grew, the children frequently took her out of her cage, wrapped her in a receiving blanket and laid her on her back, claws skyward, in the doll buggy. I often wondered, Does the chick know the difference between right side up and upside down? Jouncing over ruts and rocks in the barnyard, she remained bundled and content, while the girls danced around her singing, "I am Sam! Sam I am!" Then off they dashed, leaving Sam swaddled, claws still in the air, to wait for their return.

"Sam likes to go way high up in the sky!" Becky insisted one morning. Indeed, wings outstretched, ghost-eyes wild, our little Araucana clutched the edge of a wooden swing. "She thinks she's flying!" Jaymee squealed, giving a vigorous push that tossed the poor pullet to the ground. But Sam was on her feet instantly, fluffing indignantly, exposing hidden buttery feathers before she staggered toward the "Here chick, chick, chick" sounds from the children she'd grown to love.

Early one morning, a stray Siamese cat arrived at our kitchen door. I remember the high tail, tip twitching, the body so starved it hung over my arm like an empty sock. But most of all, it's the non-stop purr I'll never forget. The girls named him "Ping-Sing," and soon three-month-old Sam and Ping were wedged side-by-side in the doll buggy.

Their first meeting, however, wasn't easy. The cat was purring like a chain-saw, cold glitter blazing in the Siamese eyes. "Say hello!" Becky urged, shoving Sam forward. Chick and cat approached each other cautiously — Ping propelled by curiosity, Sam bewitched by vibration. Nose met beak. My fear the cat might have hunger designs on a small chicken vanished. Sam stabbed first. Ping recoiled, instantly subdued. And, from that moment on, Sam shadowed Ping as radar tracks sound, tremors of joy rippling through golden feathers as life beyond the cage, the porch rug and the doll buggy opened to her.

In the sweet warm grasses of their wanderings together,

Sam discovered squeaking beetles, buzzing flies and whirring winged ground moths. She unearthed these treasures with surprising ease and speared them with deadly accuracy. Sounds of crickets rustling among shriveled desert plants caused her neck feathers to open up like a silk umbrella. Again, at precisely the right moment, her beak struck like a javelin.

The droning bee was not such easy prey. Circling Sam's head, it teased, tormented and zoomed off. Its capture took patience and concentration, yet with Ping as her pilot and constant companion, it wasn't unusual to see our golden Araucana with the seed-pearl eyes scuttle to the edge of her boundaries and snatch the treat from the air.

September brought nature songs; popping pods from bird-of-paradise bushes rocketing seeds through the autumn air. Sam was on target like a bullet. October winds tugged mesquite beans from trees, coaxed seeds from rolling tumbleweed and orange berries from the pyracantha. Sam heard them all and snapped them up while Ping basked in sunshine and purred nearby.

November brought hay buyers; December, silver rain. Then January cast a shadow on our little Sam's life. A passerby heeded my wooden rainbow sign of success at the end of our long dirt road — ARAUCANA EGGS FOR

SALE — Blue, turquoise, buff and sea-foam green. Ready to leave with three dozen, the buyer gasped, "Where'd you find that cat?" Ping, handsome, sleek and fat now, wound love around his ankles.

"He found us," I said, longing to add, and Sam can't live without him. But what was the use? Ping was already cradled in "ol' Daddy's" arms. "Just wait till Kate sees you," he crooned. "We thought you was coyote meat." Then he turned to me. "His name's Elvis. Can't stop singin' — case you didn't notice. Always did have a danged habit of wandering off, though."

And into Sam's heart. I choked back useless argument and waved good-bye to Ping — and the joy and friendship his magic had brought to my blind chicken's life.

Sam's lonely battle with life began in earnest. Days accompanied by the sound of music were over. And since Ping had disliked chickens, Sam's encounters with her own kind had been nothing more than sounds of distant clucks and cackles.

She would have to stay caged. The only consolation for me was she'd be laying eggs soon. Would they be the beautiful colors of my other Araucana eggs? Or would they be ugly? Olive-drab like — hand grenades?

I waited for Sam to lay, but her comb stayed pea-size

and pale, unlike my fertile hens with combs and wattles draped like red wedding veils over gleaming head and throat feathers. Cheeping her misery she paced. She stopped eating. The white eyes closed and she slipped into a deep and dangerous molt, her cast-off feathers blanketing the cage floor. I had to let her out.

At first Sam hunkered down near the porch — peeping, trembling, listening? Waiting for Ping? My heart ached for her till the morning came that drew her to sounds of other chickens. I couldn't bear to watch. More than once, dagger beaks stabbed and sliced her. But Sam fought back, in her own way.

She became the barnyard fugitive. She learned to avoid clucks and squawks. She ran from sounds of barking dogs and dodged the crunch of tires. She sprinted in the opposite direction of clattering horseshoes. She spent time, instead, reclaiming the trails where she and Ping had roamed through thorny mesquite, desert grasses and dusty, vacant corrals. Once again she discovered earth's treats and treasures.

But all creatures hunger, and as the weeks passed, Sam's goal became the chicken feed and cool water inside the coop. Feigning a dust bath while the flock within bickered and ate, she listened for the ruckus to die down, signaling retreat to the nests — her chance to try. Then she arose, squeezed through the trapdoor entranceway, and once inside was permitted to eat from the feed trough alongside the few mild-mannered hens who shared with her life's misfortune — low hen in the pecking order.

At night, however, I gathered her up and placed her in her cage where she'd be safe. Although she still snuggled and gurgled with pleasure in my arms, I felt a growing resistance beneath folded wings when I placed her inside.

One summer evening after chores, I was later than usual locking the coop door for the night. To my surprise, beneath the yellow glow of lamplight hanging from the ceiling, I saw Sam perched on the feed trough sound asleep. She was one of the flock, at last, and ready to lead a life of her own.

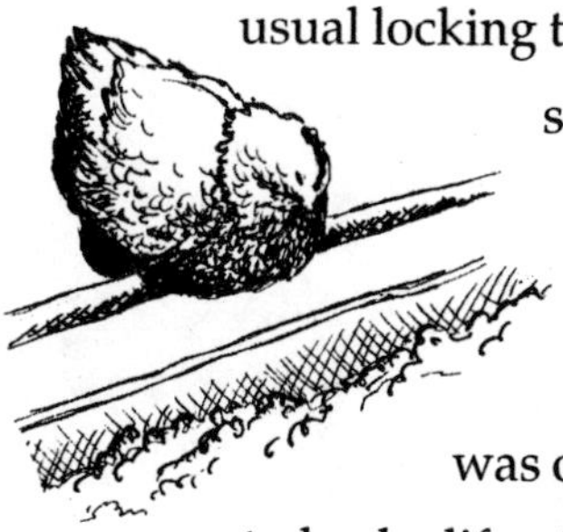

As August days grew hotter, she found her own shade beneath unused farm equipment, under log piles and huddled against cool metal water tanks. Her constant pecking and rearranging of straw-packed corners filled me with hope that she searched for a nesting place, and one day would start to lay eggs.

Sam was nearly a year old when the sixty-foot-high dust devil — a raging whirlwind of churning black sand, tumbleweed, cactus and pebbles — bore down on the barnyard and peeled back the tin roof like a can opener. It snatched eggs from nests, sucked peeps from beneath broody hens, ground sand into my eyes, then swallowed up Sam and dashed her against the tack room door. Incredibly, by the time the children and I got to her she was already on her feet, feathers puffed, head cocked, clucking bewilderment.

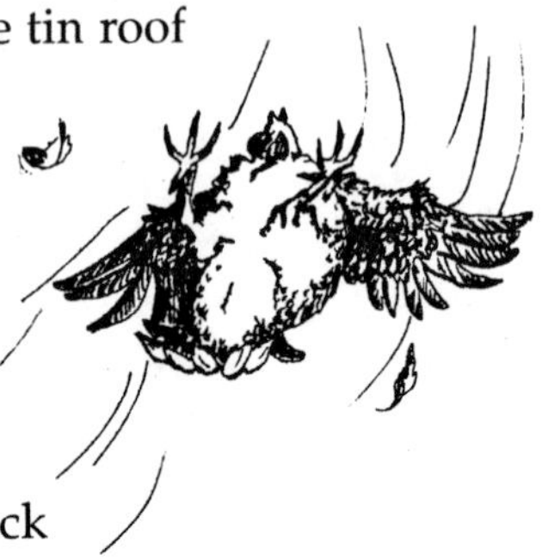

"Poor little Sam!" Becky cried.

"I can't believe she's alive," I said. "It's a miracle."

At the sound of familiar voices, Sam flapped her wings, eager to be held, to rest her golden head against my shoulder and chortle softly in my ear. I stroked the satin feathers, told her that we loved her, then handed her to Becky, who still thought it fun to carry a small chicken upsidedown.

It was September when Sam's comb pinked. At the same time, her obsession with strange places to scratch focused on an opening that led to the underside of the bucket on Bill's blue Ford tractor parked near the coop. She often crawled inside.

"She likes the shade, Mama," Becky said, and as it

grew cooler she also seemed to find it a warm, safe place to be.

Winter was coming. Bobcat, coyote and raccoon paw prints overlaid Sam's claw prints along her favorite paths through thorny mesquite, desert brush and around the henhouse. A thought nagged at my heart: How much longer will her luck hold out?

One night in late October I awoke to screeches of terror from my flock. I grabbed my flashlight and shotgun and dashed to the coop. There, in the beam of my light, glowed the eyes of a ring-tailed raccoon. It had tunneled underground, under the fence, dragged its victims out one by one — and killed them. Seven of my chickens were dead. As he set himself up to rip off my rooster's head, I fired a shot into the air. He fled.

"Did he get Sam?" Becky asked at breakfast.

Sam? Cold fear gripped me. I didn't know. Had she been roosting? I couldn't remember. Locking up chickens at night had become a routine chore. I no longer worried about Sam because she had become "just one more chicken," exactly as she wanted to be. But we still loved her. She was our pet. Was she okay?

Not until we returned to the barnyard did we see the

golden feathers scattered like aspen leaves near the bucket of the blue Ford tractor. Becky crouched to peer underneath. "Oh Mama, I don't see her," she said sadly. "Sam's gone."

In final hope I said to Bill, "Maybe she's way underneath the bucket, between the wooden supports." He climbed up into the tractor cab and turned the key. Hydraulics whined and the giant shovel rose from its resting place.

That's when I saw them — four little mud-green eggs cradled in a straw-banked nest. A gift from Sam — the promise of magic that had been there all along, the story of life from beginning to end with all its struggles and miracles. A mere chicken Sam might have been, but she showed us that all life is precious. At last I was sure I'd done the right thing.

Bill looked down at me, a tease crinkling the corners of his eyes. "What are you going to do?" he called. "Hatch them?"

"Of course!" I said, suddenly aware that olive drab didn't seem so ugly any more. But deep in my heart I knew there could be only one golden chicken with seed-pearl eyes. I'd held her life in my hand.

September 16, 1969

Mary Riley arrived on moccasin-clad feet. She was a soft spoken woman, and it would be until evening before would learn that she was Chief Councilwoman and a long-time elder of the White River Apaches. From our kitchen door Becky and I watched the beautiful group of Indian people coming: Mary, her niece and several other very large women with full skirts billowing like colorful sails seemed to float toward the ranch down our long dirt road. Two young children and a mixed-breed dog skipped alongside them. There was a quiet man, somebody's uncle, someone to drive an ancient pickup left at the gate. He said nothing. They carried baskets woven from bear grass, which grows in many areas of southeastern Arizona, and, asked if they could gather piñon nuts from our western acorn trees. "Pinon nuts used to be a favorite for bread-baking among my people," Mary said. Today, however, "The nuts are a treat as special as candy for no one wants to take the time to pick them," she said sadly. "They have become lazy."

At noon, I insisted they have some lemonade and lunch, and rest in the shade of our giant cottonwood tree. Mary loved to chat. She told me she had been to Washington many times as representative for her tribe and she had decorated fourteen presidents with a carved medallion symbolic of her people. From a pocket somewhere in her voluminous skirt, she produced a picture of herself in a parade with Franklin Delano Roosevelt.

While we talked, Mary's nine-year-old nephew suddenly jumped on one of our more skittish horses — bareback! Without saddle or bridal he loped the horse around the pasture with only the gentlest pressure of his knees and bare hands. After that, Becky followed him around all day long, sharing her sandwich and a favorite kitten, and helping gather nuts off the ground while he climbed trees.

Before they left, Mary told Bill he was going to have another daughter. How does she know? I wondered. Bill was so pleased, he gave Mary's nephew a kitten to take home with him. As a matter of fact, he tried to give Mary the whole litter but she assured him one cat *was enough. "Maybe next time," she said.*

THE UGLIEST CAT IN THE WORLD

The first time I ever saw Smoky, she was on fire. My three children and I had just arrived at the dump outside our Arizona desert town to burn the weekly trash. As we approached the smoldering pit, we heard the most mournful cries of a cat entombed in the smoking rubble below.

Suddenly a large cardboard box, which had been wired shut, burst into flames and exploded. With a long, piercing meow, the animal imprisoned within shot into the air like a flaming rocket and dropped into the ash-filled crater.

"Oh Mama, do something!" three-year-old Jaymee cried as she and Becky, age six, leaned over the smoking hole.

"It can't possibly still be alive," said Scott. But the ashes moved and a tiny kitten, charred almost beyond recognition, miraculously struggled to the surface and crawled toward us in agony.

"I'll get her!" Scott yelled. As he stood knee-deep in

ashes and wrapped the kitten in my bandanna, I wondered why it didn't cry from the added pain. Later we learned we had heard its last meow only moments before.

Back at our ranch, we were doctoring the kitten when my husband, Bill, came in, weary from a long day of fence mending.

"Daddy! We found a burned-up kitty," Jaymee announced.

When he saw our patient, that familiar "Oh, no, not again!" look crossed his face. This wasn't the first time we had greeted him with an injured animal. Though Bill always grumbled, he couldn't bear to see any living creature suffer. So he helped by building cages, perches, pens and splints for the skunks, rabbits and birds we brought home. This was different, however. This was a cat. And Bill, very definitely, did not like cats.

What's more, this was no ordinary cat. Where fur had been, blisters and a sticky black gum remained. Her ears were gone. Her tail was cooked to the bone. Gone were the claws that would have snatched some unsuspecting mouse. Gone were the little paw pads that would have left telltale tracks on the hoods of our dusty cars and trucks. Nothing that resembled a cat was left — except for two huge cobalt-blue eyes begging for help.

What could we do?

Suddenly I remembered our aloe vera plant and its supposed healing power on burns. So we peeled the leaves, swathed the kitten in slimy aloe strips and gauze bandages, and placed her in Jaymee's Easter basket. All we could see was her tiny face, like a butterfly waiting to emerge from its silk cocoon.

Her tongue was severely burned, and the inside of her mouth was so blistered that she couldn't lap, so we fed her milk and water with an eyedropper. After a while, she began eating by herself.

We named the kitten Smoky.

Three weeks later, the aloe plant was bare. Now we coated Smoky with a salve instead that turned her body a curious shade of green. Her tail dropped off. Not a hair remained, but the children and I adored her.

Bill didn't. And Smoky despised him. The reason? He was a pipe smoker, and pipe smokers come armed with matches and butane lighters that flashed and burned. Every time he lit up, Smoky panicked, knocking over his coffee cup and lamps before fleeing into the open air duct in the spare bedroom.

"Can't I have any peace around here?" he'd groan.

In time, Smoky became more tolerant of the pipe and its owner. She'd lie on the sofa and glare at Bill as he puffed away. One day he looked at me and chuckled, "Damn cat makes me feel guilty."

As Smoky's health improved, we marveled at her patience with the girls, who dressed her in doll clothes and bonnets so the "no ears" wouldn't show. Then they held her up to the mirror so she could see "how pretty" she was.

By the end of her first year, Smoky resembled a well-used welding glove. Scott was now famous among his friends for owning the ugliest pet in the county — probably the world.

Smoky longed to play outside where the sounds of birds, chickens and ground squirrels tempted her. When it was time to feed our outdoor pets, including our Mexican lobo, the occasional skunks and assorted lizards, she sat inside, spellbound, with her nose pressed against the window. It was the barn cats, however, that caused her tiny body to tremble with eagerness. But since she

had no claws for protection, we couldn't let her go outside unwatched.

Sometimes we took Smoky out on the front porch when other animals weren't around. If she was lucky, an unsuspecting beetle or June bug would make the mistake of strolling across the concrete. Smoky would stalk, bat and toss the bug until it flipped onto its back where, one hopes, it died of fright before she ate it.

Slowly, oddly, Bill became the one she cared for the most. And before long, I noticed a change in him. He rarely smoked in the house now, and one winter night, to my astonishment, I found him sitting in his chair with the leathery little cat curled up on his lap. Before I could comment, he mumbled a curt, "She's probably cold — no fur you know."

But Smoky, I reminded myself, liked the touch of cold. Didn't she sleep in front of air ducts and on the cold Mexican-tile floor?

Perhaps Bill was starting to like this strange-looking animal just a bit.

Not everyone shared our feelings for Smoky, especially those who had never seen her. Rumors reached a group of self-appointed animal protectors, and one day one of them arrived at our door.

"I've had numerous calls and letters from so many

people," the woman said. "They are concerned about a poor little burned-up cat you have in your house. They say," her voice dropped an octave, "she's suffering. Perhaps she should be put out of her misery?"

I was furious. Bill was even more so. "Burned she was," he said, "but suffering? Look for yourself!"

"Here kitty," I called. No Smoky. "She's probably hiding," I said, but our guest didn't answer. When I turned and looked at her, the woman's skin was gray, her mouth hung open and two fingers pointed.

Magnified tenfold in all her naked splendor, Smoky glowered at our visitor from her hiding place behind our 150-gallon aquarium. Instead of the "poor little burned-up suffering creature" the woman expected to see, tyrannosaurus Smoky leered at her through the green aquatic maze. Her open jaws exposed saber-like fangs that glinted menacingly in the neon light. Moments later the woman hurried out the door — smiling now, a little embarrassed and greatly relieved.

During Smoky's second year, a miraculous thing happened. She began growing fur. Tiny white hairs, softer and finer than the down on a chick, gradually grew over three inches long, transforming our ugly little cat into a wispy puff of smoke.

Bill continued to enjoy her company, though the two

made an incongruous pair — the big weather-worn rancher driving around with an unlit pipe clenched between his teeth, accompanied by the tiny white ball of fluff. When he got out of the truck to check the cattle, he left the air conditioner on Maximum/Cold for her comfort. Her blue eyes watered, the pink nose ran, but she sat there, unblinking, in ecstasy. Other times, he picked her up and, holding her close against his denim jacket, took her along.

Smoky was three years old on the day she went with Bill to look for a missing calf. Searching for hours, he would leave the truck door open when he got out to look. The pastures were parched and crisp with dried grasses and tumbleweed. A storm loomed on the horizon, and still no calf. Discouraged, without thinking, Bill reached into his pocket for his lighter and spun the wheel. A spark shot to the ground and, in seconds, the field was on fire.

Frantic, Bill didn't think about the cat. Only after the fire was under control and the calf found did he return home — and remember.

"Smoky!" he cried. "She must have jumped out of the truck! Did she come home?"

No. And we knew she'd never find her way home from two miles away. To make matters worse, it had started to rain so hard we couldn't go out to look for her.

Bill was distraught, blaming himself. We spent the next day searching, wishing she could meow for help, and knowing she'd be helpless against predators. It was no use.

Two weeks later Smoky still wasn't home. We were afraid she was dead by now, for the rainy season had begun, and the hawks, wolves and coyotes had families to feed.

Then came the biggest rainstorm our region had had in fifty years. By morning, flood waters stretched for miles, marooning wildlife and cattle on scattered islands of higher ground. Frightened rabbits, raccoons, squirrels and desert rats waited for the water to subside, while Bill and Scott waded knee-deep, carrying bawling calves back to their mamas and safety.

The girls and I were watching intently when suddenly Jaymee shouted, "Daddy! There's a poor little rabbit over there. Can you get it?"

Bill waded to the spot where the animal lay, but when he reached out to help the tiny creature, it seemed to shrink back in fear. "I don't believe it," Bill cried. "It's Smoky!" His voice broke. "Little Smoky!"

My eyes ached with tears when that pathetic little cat crawled into the outstretched hands of the man she had grown to love. He pressed her shivering body to his chest, talked to her softly, and gently wiped the mud from her face. All the while her blue eyes fastened on his with unspoken understanding. He was forgiven.

Smoky came home again. The patience she showed as we shampooed her astounded us. We fed her scrambled eggs and ice cream, and to our joy she seemed to get well.

But Smoky had never really been strong. One morning when she was barely four years old, we found her limp in Bill's chair. Her heart had simply stopped.

As I wrapped her tiny body in one of Bill's red neckerchiefs and placed her in a child's shoe box, I thought about the many things our precious Smoky had taught us — things about trust, affection and struggling against the odds when everything says you can't win. She reminded us that it's not what's outside that counts — it's what's inside, deep in our hearts.

That's why Smoky will always be in my heart. And why, to me, she will always be the most beautiful cat in the world.

July 4, 1974

We welcome many guests, old friends, who love to visit the ranch. This means cooking for even more than the usual nine or ten. At the end of each day I have prepared between twenty-five and forty meals. It's lucky I like to cook because I might as well be running a restaurant.

We have a little guest house I call "The Outpost." It's about ten feet from my chicken house. This week Tom and Martha Summers came from California for a few days and nights. Tom's a radio ham and was a Sigma Nu fraternity brother of Bill's at Lehigh.

Tom looked so tired each morning, I wondered if the altitude gave him a headache. The elevation of Singing Valley Ranch is 4500 feet. Well, I discovered his head had nothing to do with his fatigue.

This morning before they left, Tom, looking more haggard than ever, brought a tape recording to the breakfast table. We couldn't wait to hear what he was going to play. "The hour . . ." said the voice in the box, Tom's voice, "is exactly 4:00 A.M. I long for sleep. But it's over. May I present, 'Sleepless Nights at Singing Valley'?" The recording that followed featured my half-grown roosters practicing their newly discovered talent , the art of crowing, throughout breakfast. It seems Tom's window was ten feet from the coop, and to make matters worse I had made the novice's mistake of ordering one hundred "straight-run" chicks that had grown into – fifty hens and fifty ROOSTERS – instead of the one hundred hens I wanted.

Like Tom, Bill isn't happy about this. "You're going to have to butcher the boys," he grumbled.

Me? Butcher? He's got to be kidding. If Tom were staying longer, he'd probably be more than happy to do the job. Meanwhile, I'll ask a neighbor to do the job.

A ROOSTER NAMED BENEDICT

"Cereal again?" Bill scowled at the heaping bowlful placed in front of him. "It looks just like what I fed those yearling bulls an hour ago . . ."

"I'm sorry, honey," I said, "but we ran out of eggs again! If we had our own chickens, this wouldn't happen all the time."

"But we're ranchers," he muttered. "Ranchers raise cattle. Farmers raise chickens."

When you live on an Arizona ranch many miles from the nearest store, no eggs is a disaster. Our whole family loved eggs, especially Bill. He had them every morning — poached, fried or scrambled. But most of all he loved eggs Benedict.

And I loved chickens, which is why I wanted some of our own. Ever since we'd bought the ranch, my mind had been filled with storybook images of a little red hen, four golden chicks and a magnificent rooster perched on a weather vane, welcoming the sunrise. "If we had our own chickens," I again reminded Bill, "we'd never ever run out of eggs!"

He'd heard all this before. Now he heaved a sigh of resignation. I hugged him, knowing I'd won.

While Bill proceeded to erect a chicken coop and order a weather vane, I pored through poultry catalogs with the children. A neighbor suggested buying 100 chicks. "With your big family you'll need that many for sure," he said, "and you can sell all the extras."

Hatcheries, I learned, mail one extra chick for every twenty-five ordered — consolation for the few that get squashed in shipping. What a relief it was that all 104 of ours survived and soon were housed under a heat lamp on our kitchen floor. For variety, I'd ordered Leghorns, Plymouth Rocks, Rhode Island Reds and — my favorite of all — Araucanas. Once grown, Araucanas lay blue, buff, olive-green and turquoise eggs. "Every day will be Easter!" I told the children.

Right away we noticed one Araucana was bigger and bossier than the rest. Terror and confusion reigned as she chased the others from food and water. The poultry book warned: "There is always a dominant hen in a flock who fights to maintain her position as 'number one in the pecking order.'" This big chick, I decided, was "number one."

Wondering if extra handling might calm her, I cupped

the chick in my hands, carried her around and talked softly to her. To my surprise, this worked. The frantic cheeping stopped, the eyelids closed, and the tiny heart knocking at my palms finally slowed down. I also fed the chick by herself, hoping she'd eat her fill and one day lay the biggest eggs of all. In anticipation of her first egg, Bill named her Benedictine.

Six months after the chicks were delivered, our assumption that all were females proved to be flawed: We had fifty-two roosters and fifty-two hens. That many roosters heralding the dawn was a whole lot more than we could take. So we pruned the flock to one rooster — the big one, Benedictine. I renamed him Benedict.

Gradually, Benedict grew to the size of a small turkey. He was young, proud, magnificent. As he matured, his comb and wattles deepened to a rich scarlet. He sported a glorious multicolored cape and streaming tail feathers that flashed red, green, yellow and glistening onyx in the Arizona sunshine. His claws were nearly as large as my hands, and his golden spurs, tipped with razor-sharp talons, glinted on the backs of his legs.

Benedict became my pet. He sought attention by untying my sneaker laces and gargling his pleasure when I produced a cookie or peanut-butter treat. He won Best of Show at the county fair, and in my arms he rested quietly, showing an unusual tameness for a rooster. He loved and trusted me. I loved and trusted him.

Long before the end of their first year, our Araucana hens were laying colored eggs, which sold for three dollars a dozen. Meanwhile, virile Benedict was making certain every egg was fertilized, and local farmers and 4-H enthusiasts sought those eggs for hatching to replenish their own flocks. With Benedict's help, my chickens were paying their way.

At age three, however, his status as the only rooster began going to his head. Previously, Benedict had loved the company of the hens. Now, acting like the king of the roost, he started attacking any hen who dared to share his throne, which was the uppermost perch. If a hen tried to snatch a kernel of cracked corn from the feeder before he was finished, Benedict would pin her to the ground, hold fast with his terrible talons, and stab her repeatedly with his dagger-like beak.

"You shoulda kept more than one rooster," said my neighbor. "Too much breeding's addled his brain."

Soon Benedict started turning on me as well. Gone was the old trust, the contented clucking, cookie searching and plucking at my sneaker laces. Now, following me from nest to nest, he scolded, thumped his feet and made ghoulish hissing sounds. Knowing his long, sharp beak could skewer my leg, I was forced to enter the coop armed with a broom, rake or pitchfork. Even then, when his comb and wattles turned from scarlet to purple, weapons were useless. I ran.

Then one night I awakened to a chaotic squawking and screeching from the coop. Grabbing a flashlight and our shotgun, I dashed up the trail toward my flock. There, in the beam of my light, glowed the evil eyes of a ring-tailed raccoon which had tunneled into the coop. Half a dozen hens were already dead, and others lay mortally wounded. Now the raccoon clutched Benedict in his horrible claws and was preparing to rip off his head.

Though I feared Benedict, I still loved him. Gripping the flashlight between my knees, I closed my eyes and fired into the air. When I looked again, the raccoon was barreling off into the mesquite. Benedict lay still, gasping for air, his eyes wild with terror. I knelt beside him, stroked the satin feathers, and talked softly to him. Gradually he calmed down.

From that night on, I had my old Benedict back again. When we walked together from nest to nest, he gurgled approval as I filled my basket with eggs. He even puffed himself up grandly when I presented him with ten new hens to replace those he'd lost to the raccoon.

As the years passed, Benedict went faithfully about his duties. Then something turned his world — and mine — upside down. One of his hens became "broody," tired of laying. She wanted to hatch eggs instead, and insisted on taking over the "favorite nest," a single box preferred by as many as a dozen different hens. Unable to gain access to this coveted spot, the other hens dropped their eggs on the concrete floor.

For some reason, "Broody" inspired in Benedict a passion beyond reason. By the hour he would pace under her nest. He refused to eat. He lost his voice. He's getting old, senile and mixed up, I thought. Then he decided to chase the more docile hens out of the other nests.

Production plunged.

To make matters worse, Benedict, now ten years old, was slowing down. The hens, detecting this, started pecking at him and pulling out his wing, tail and back feathers. Benedict sank lower and lower with each attack.

For his own protection, I decided to put him in a cage until his sores healed. I also bought two young roosters to keep the flock occupied. Broody hatched four eggs and I moved her and her chicks to the yard by our house.

When I returned Benedict to the flock, he searched for Broody for days, peering into her previous nest again and again. At the same time, he was trying to fight off the younger roosters and dominant hens. Eventually Benedict's searching ceased and he retired to a distant corner of the chicken yard by day. I was too busy to notice his constant molting and loss of appetite, and sadly I never noticed his morning greeting had ceased and he clung to the bottom rung of the roost at night.

Instead, I enjoyed watching Broody and her four tiny chicks, particularly the one that was different from the others. "Mama, she's almost purple," said Jaymee. "I'm going to name her Violet."

From the start, Violet was unusual. She never grew a comb or wattles, the measures of a hen's fertility. She couldn't cluck, but instead peeped and chattered. Like a child she jumped into doll buggies and waited for a ride. She sat on the swing until someone pushed. She pecked at boots and shoes until one of us picked her up.

At two, when Violet still hadn't laid an egg, the idea came to me that perhaps a rooster around might help. Using one of the younger ones was out of the question — I was afraid of them and couldn't catch them anyway. Benedict! I thought.

I hurried to the coop to get him. When I saw him in the darkness of the chicken house, I was saddened beyond words. With his beak open and eyes closed, his head and neck hung down like a long forgotten-rope.

Scarcely a feather remained on his twelve-year-old body, and his graying flesh was mapped in purple and green bruises, mute evidence of the constant abuse he endured from nagging hens. How could you let this happen! I scolded myself. Because he was old and ugly? Because you were too busy to care? "Benedict," I murmured, "Please don't be dead."

At the sound of my voice he stirred, teetering dangerously on that bottom roost. I wrapped my arms around him and lifted him carefully. When he rested his head against my shoulder I couldn't help remembering how *beautiful* he was — when he was young.

When I reached the yard to put him down, he lay quietly, savoring the touch of soft grass beneath his wrinkled skin and blinking from the glare of the bright Arizona sun. After a bit, he struggled to stand. My heart ached for him — until he saw Violet.

She was a beautiful hen now, plump and round in all the right places. His head sprang up and down, and the tired eyes brightened.

I could see his heart pounding beneath the sunken ribs, fighting to loosen the chains of age. Alive with desire, he thumped his feet, clacked his beak, lifted his head — and for the first time in years, crowed! Then my ugly old rooster lurched through the tumbleweeds in pursuit of his new love. By nightfall, with Violet nestled at his side, Benedict was perching contentedly on the lowest branch of a tree in our yard

For two glorious weeks, Benedict enjoyed an idyllic life with Violet. They took dust baths together, scratched for worms and squabbled over bugs. I'd never seen him eat so well and I put vitamins in his food hoping to build him up a little. Before long, his arrogant strut of long ago returned, and a shimmering veil of opalescent down began to conceal the battered flesh. He also started welcoming dawn with raspy song.

Two weeks, however, was all Benedict had left. When I went out one morning to feed them, I found him motionless on the ground beneath that branch he'd shared with Violet. I tried to comfort myself with the thought, *He died happy.*

Mourning her loss, Violet spent her days searching and peeping her sorrow. She grew thin and began losing her feathers. Twelve days later, she laid her first and only egg — and died. I reasoned there had been internal complications, but Jaymee was sure Violet had died of a broken heart.

"Violet and Benedict's baby," Jaymee cried, picking up the large turquoise egg lying on the front doormat. "It's in here, Mama."

We placed the egg in our commercial brooder. Twenty-one days later Omelette hatched. He was an adorable chick. The image of his father, he grew into the proudest of roosters. He developed a scarlet comb and wattles, rainbow-tinted tail feathers, copper-colored eyes, and golden spurs on his heels. He carried on the Benedict dynasty for years.

When the day came that Omelette, too, grew old, ugly

and confused, I remembered Benedict. And I took the time to stroke Omelette's ancient, torn feathers and talk to him. Just to let the old rooster know that he, too, was special.

September 21, 1975

Becky started school today. First grade. There are thirty-three children in the McNeal school, grades K-8. Everyone has recess at the same time. All ages play baseball, kick-ball, jacks, soccer and jump-rope together. The older kids watch out for the little ones, and a shy child is taken by the hand and brought in to play with everybody.

The principal's name is Fred Stolp. He not only attended the McNeal School himself when he was a little boy, but has been head teacher there for thirty-five years, ever since World War II when he was in the Army Air Corps. The children love him.

"Mr. Stolp" has a paddle that hangs on the wall behind his desk. It is always the first thing the students show the new kids in school. Fred has never used it. He doesn't have to. The children respect him. And they learn. The majority of children who graduate from the McNeal Elementary School excel in high school and go on to college because they have learned good study habits from kindergarten on where they were enforced. If they don't have good manners when they come to school, they learn them quickly. But above all, they learn to listen.

The Mexican children are not allowed to speak Spanish in school. (I think they do because Becky understands lots of it and knows many words after only one year.) Even on the playground they are supposed to speak English. The Mexican parents are thrilled. They came to this country to be Americans. They are proud of their Mexican descent and struggle to learn English themselves. "How else will my children learn?" one Mexican lady asked me in faltering English. "My children are American. They must learn to speak like an American."

Children attending the McNeal school have nearly perfect yearly attendance. I asked Becky, "How come?" All my other kids missed lots of school. Becky looked at me, eyes huge. "Mr. Stolp says the only legitimate reason for missing a day of school is a death in the family." Does she even know the meaning of the word — legitimate?

A LITTLE ON THE WILD SIDE

Hunger stalks the parched Arizona mountains and winter rangelands. Coyotes howl their distress. Raccoons plunder my chicken coop, and feral dogs lust after our newborn calves. But it is the piteous cries of wild cats, solo wanderers of the desert, that tear at my heart. Abandoned, no place to call home, these castaways revert to a primal life and a singular culture of their own, yet every year when hard times come they seek food and shelter in the barns and outbuildings of our cattle ranch and farm.

One cold March morning, I was milking our dairy cow while five fat, domestic barn cats rubbed against my jeans, impatient to be fed. They don't even know what hunger is, I thought, attempting to count the skeletal, untouchable wild cats cringing in dark corners, cowering behind feed bins, and pacing rafters veiled in spider webs that spanned the barn like trapeze nets. Ragged fur of black, grey and tortoise-shell had camouflaged these homeless creatures well against desert predators, but starvation had taken its toll. Most were ill. Many were pregnant. Some were hideously scarred, mute evidence of desperate battles for life. I counted at least fifteen; plus our five pets that made twenty cats. Somehow both wild and tame knew it was feeding time.

Suddenly, Jaymee, the youngest of our six children, rushed in to the barn cupping a snow-white newborn kitten in her hands. "It fell out of the nest its mama made up in the palm tree," she cried. "All its brothers and sisters are dead. Something killed them!"

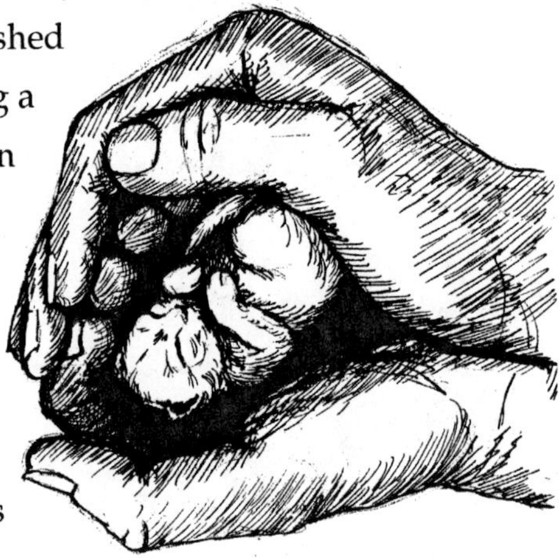

Yesterday morning I'd spotted another unfamiliar cat huddled in the shadows behind a bale of hay. Unlike most wild cats, she was easy to see because bright white patches of fur flashed among her varied calicos, making her an easy target for any predator. Fear smoldered in her remaining yellow eye. She was pregnant. Today she was gone.

"I'll bet the great horned owl got them, honey," I said, wondering how the tiny creature in her hands had escaped the ripping talons and murderous hooked beak of this deadly night predator. The hours-old kitten nuzzled Jaymee's palms and mewed piteously. "You've got to find its mother," I said. "It needs to nurse."

"She's dead too!" Jaymee fastened her brown eyes on mine. "Oh, Mama. I saw her. What are we going to do?"

Jaymee had watched us struggle to keep orphaned calves and foals alive. Now she'd found something just the right size for a six-year-old, a wild thing, a precious scrap of life she could hold, love and take care of by herself. She hugged it to her cheek and in a voice filled with sadness said, "Without a mama, it'll die, won't it?"

"Yes," I answered softly. "It'll take a miracle to save it."

I sighed, poured warm, foaming milk laced with antibiotics into several shallow bowls, then filled two trays with cat chow and turned again to Jaymee. "Let's take your kitty in the house," I said, "and see what's best to do."

"We have to make a miracle, don't we, Mama?"

"Only God makes miracles."

"But can't I help?"

I hugged her. "You can try."

In the kitchen we wrapped the tiny creature in a lamb's wool mitten and fed it diluted milk with an eye dropper. Then we placed it in a round, four-egg-capacity incubator we kept on hand to hatch chicks of rare breed hens all year round. It had a clear plastic dome on top so we could see inside.

"Can I keep it in my room?" Jaymee asked.

I nodded. "But — don't tell Daddy about it just yet. You know how he feels about cats."

I, too, hoped for a miracle, but doubt filled my heart. This tiny creature needed a mother cat, not a six-year-old child. And what if it did live? Jaymee would get attached and the call of the wild might win in the end anyway. It would take off and she'd be heartbroken. Most of these cats were descendants of previous throwaways and had never known the touch of man. They had become accustomed to an untamed life, the life of a fugitive, in which survival depended on cunning, independence and solitary wandering. But for now, so much hope shone in my little girl's eyes, I had to help.

Bill, unlit pipe clenched between his teeth, came in for breakfast, his wrists raked with angry, bleeding scratches and welts. "I found another litter of strays in the manure spreader," he said. "That mother wanted to kill me — vicious as any wild animal I've ever seen! And seven kittens, eyes barely open, yowled, hissed, spit and tried to bite me like full grown pumas. I made the mistake of trying to pull them out barehanded — finally had to put on welding gloves to grab 'em, and hold the mother back with a broom." I drenched his arms with iodine after he assured me, begrudgingly, that he'd put the kittens in a box where they'd be safe and the mother could find them.

Sooner or later Bill would find out about Jaymee's kitten, so I hoped I'd heard the last of the cat problems for the morning. But no. He gulped his coffee and began again: "Darn mice chewed holes in nearly every sack of grain in the barn. You'd think our cats could keep them under control. That's why we have them, but they have to spend all their time chasing off those wild ones. They hate them. I've never seen so many . . . nesting all over the place, in the irrigation pipes, chimneys, the farm machinery, fifteen feet in the air on windmill platforms . . ." And twenty feet high in a palm tree, I mused.

"Maybe if you left the feed room door open at night, the wild cats could get in and catch the mice," I offered brightly.

He shot me a quick glance. "Think what else could get in. Rain! Raccoons! Rattlers! The owls'll get 'em eventually, I suppose. They can fly in under the eaves."

"I think the owls are getting full on cats," I countered.

"Not fast enough for me," he said. "Those miserable wild things look sick. They could be carrying rabies! Or ringworm that could spread to the cattle!"

Sometimes nature seemed cruel. Year after year these wild cats reproduced their own kind in the wilderness. They struggled for survival against predators, illness and starvation. Eventually, they wandered onto our ranch where I fattened them up — and the owls ate them.

That night, Jaymee and Becky, her nine-year-old sister, fed the tiny kitten and returned it to the incubator that glowed on their bedside table like a miniature flying saucer with a tiny space traveler inside. I heard Becky whisper to Jaymee, "I counted twenty-two wild cats in the barn this morning. That doesn't include Cally, Whiskey, Blueberry, Mickey or Floyd. Daddy's having a conniption."

"Does he know we really have twenty-three?" Jaymee asked.

"Not yet."

"Who's going to tell him?"

"Not me," said Becky, "but he'll find out."

Ten days later the kitten's eyes opened, and Jaymee named it Miracle. "It's a girl," she announced at dinner that night.

"Aren't they always?" said Bill, his eyebrows perfect pup tents as he scowled at me. Jaymee had shown him the kitten in the incubator the day before. When she said, "Doesn't it look like the littlest astronaut in the world, Daddy?" what could he say? But I knew he wasn't happy.

Miracle. There could be no other name for this tiny pink-nosed, blue-eyed star in Jaymee's life. However, when I looked at her fur, white as milkweed down except for the copper patch of calico behind her left ear, I thought about the dark that waits with "stars" of its own —

coyotes, raccoons and great horned owls. At the same time, I knew we couldn't keep this kitten in the house forever.

Somehow, Miracle would have to become a domestic cat, a barn cat. Meanwhile, worries and problems haunted me. Instead of sleeping prettily in her own bed, Miracle hid in closets and behind drapes. After long searches we found her skulking in back of the aquarium and bookshelves, in Bill's extra pair of boots, or snoozing under beds and sofas. The household question became, "Where's Miracle?"

Then there was Bill. He didn't like cats in the house. A newborn trapped in an incubator was one thing. But, when Miracle was two weeks old I noticed him trying to avoid the kitten's bewitching jewel-like eyes, muttering, "She's getting bigger." At last the morning came when he caught Miracle skydiving from the drapes. That afternoon she mastered free-flying from curtains to lampshades, and by nightfall the lazy Susan on the kitchen table became a splendid launching pad for a white fur-glazed rocket aimed at shelves, counters and destinations unknown. On the day when she spiraled up Bill's jeans with claws unsheathed, life for Miracle took a nose dive. The enclosed back porch became her new home.

For a while she perched on the windowsill, seemingly content to bat at dusty sunbeams or track a leaf scuttling across the parched fields outside. But more often, I noticed an accusing loneliness in the deep blue eyes, a sudden dilation of black pupils or an anxious tail twitching a warning. Miracle was carving dreams — wild cat dreams — of an unmapped world with all its tempting possibilities beyond the glassed-in porch.

Bonded to Jaymee from her earliest hours, Miracle seemed unaware she was a cat. "'Mirry's afraid of cats," Jaymee said. "She thinks she's a person." Indeed, the kitten liked to eat on the kitchen table when Bill wasn't around. She thrilled at rides in the pickup on Jaymee's lap. She loved being brushed, but she never learned to wash herself like domestic cats do. We wondered if wild cats didn't bathe. Regardless, Jaymee gave her baths to keep her white, and unlike most cats, Miracle loved her bath — especially the blow-dryer.

Although we offered Miracle marbles, jacks and fluffy ribbons to play with, she wasn't interested and waited impatiently for us to take her outdoors instead. Bursting with curiosity, she leaped through hay buyers' truck windows, darted into the alfalfa fields and crouched outside my chicken coop trembling with desire at the sight of 200 peeps. She had to be watched, and I was always relieved when the children brought her back inside where she curled up like a pretty white powder puff and purred happily on Jaymee's lap until "porch time."

In the happy hunting grounds of my imagination, it was hard to imagine that anything so precious might really have wild cat blood running through her veins, natural wanderlust and instincts that could one day tempt her to prey on baby creatures and birds. We wanted Miracle to be different, the stay-in-the-house-cat variety addicted to catnip. After all, she loved being read to, sharing popsicles, and being caressed on that patch of calico behind her left ear by a little girl who loved her. I prayed she'd stay that way, but at the age of seven months, the nighttime yowling began.

"She sees things in the dark that we can't see," said Jaymee at breakfast. "Secrets and—"

"—tomcats!" said Bill, stiff-necked and grouchy from sleeping with his head under the pillow to block out Miracle's cries. "Darn cat," he grumbled, giving me a frosty look. The yowling grew worse. Although deep down I knew better, I liked to think the little cat was simply lonely for Jaymee.

Jaymee had ideas of her own. "Maybe if Mirry had a friend?" she suggested. "Blueberry's going to have kittens. Maybe . . ."

Bill didn't have to say no. A raised eyebrow, a steely glance or a deeper drag on his pipe spoke louder than words. We all knew there'd be no "friend" on the porch for Miracle.

One evening Bill came in for dinner with a handful of rattlesnake rattles. "We found a nest of more than fifty of the critters over at Cowan's ranch," he said, locking his rifle in the gun cabinet and tossing the rattles onto the kitchen table. He selected the biggest, a set with thirteen rattles, and shook it. Instantly Miracle's pink nose was pressed against the kitchen window. Her back arched. Flinty eyes sparked.

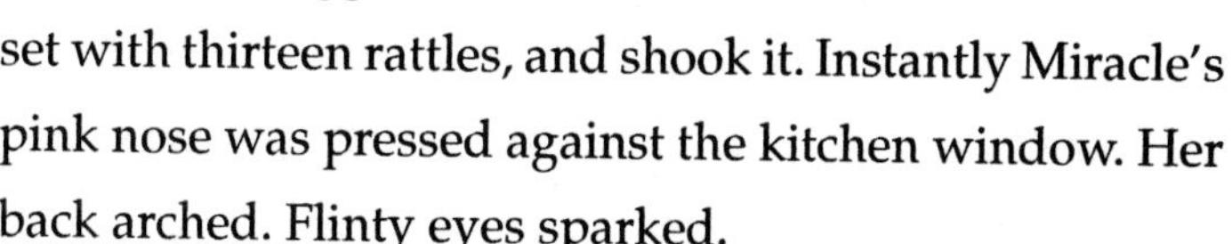

"Oh, Daddy. Can Mirry have one to play with?" Jaymee asked.

"Sure," he said. "Why not?"

The little cat bristled and pounced. No boring toy this. Something far more interesting. A nudge? A danger? A thrill instilled from the wildcat world? In seconds, the rattles were clicking and skittering across the slick tile floor like a hockey puck, Miracle in pursuit executing hairpin turns, her hindquarters jackknifing like our cattle trailer did when Bill had to slam on the brakes to avoid hitting a rabbit. For a while, the yowls in the night diminished as our little white cat honed her latent feline skills — on rattlesnake rattles.

We began leaving Miracle outside all day, in the hope she would sleep better at night. She did, and we noticed something else too. Instead of hiding in the daylight as wildcats do, Miracle stayed in view. Like a little white ghost, she shinnied up trees, soared among branches and prowled around my chicken house. Maybe, I thought, if we were lucky, she'll become a domestic cat after all. Already she always came when Jaymee called.

One of Miracle's favorite places was the barn where Bill and our son, Scott, were halter-breaking young bulls for a cattle show. There she tried to make friends with our tame cats. She would always walk around them first, but her hair stood straight up on the ridge of her back and she'd hiss. Then, feeling a little braver, she would reach out cautiously, tap a tail and run. But her curiosity when it came to the illusive wild cats worried me. She was strangely attracted to them, drawn soundlessly into dark corners, haystacks and high up on barn rafters where our domestic cats never went. Not a single hair stood on end. No yowling. No hissing. Instead, she seemed to enjoy a silent communication, a natural kinship, a bonding beyond our understanding before she moved on to another.

Most of all Miracle enjoyed the feed room where, instead of catching mice, she played with them until they died of fright. Then she carried them tenderly to the porch door and lined them up like Tootsie Rolls.

"See, Daddy, she's not just another wildcat like you thought she'd be," Jaymee said. "She's doing a good job. But why doesn't she eat the mice like other cats do?" She wrinkled her nose.

"Because you and Mama feed her so much she doesn't have to."

Jaymee scooped Miracle from the ground and looked her in the eye. "You'd never kill anything and eat it, would you, Mirry?" she murmured. The small white cat cuddled up in the arms of the little girl she loved, and purred.

One day I discovered a round, oozing sore on Miracle's forehead. At first I suspected she'd been hurt until blisters and circles erupted on Jaymee's cheeks, arms and around her neck as well.

"Ringworm," said the vet after examining both cat and child under the diagnostic "blue-light," where the pair glittered like glowworms on a summer night. "You'll have to treat them with tincture of green soap and antibiotic salve for several weeks; and, by the way, warn Bill to watch those bulls. This strain is highly contagious."

That night when Bill came in for supper, beat, I could tell it was already too late.

"Two of the show bulls have ringworm," he said.

I thought of his disappointment, the quarantine, the extra hours of work, the cost of antibiotics and lime/sulfur dips for animals weighing close to 2000 pounds, and "the darn wild cats" that had brought the disease onto the ranch, and even gave it to Miracle, who in turn transmitted it to Jaymee. I wanted to say, "I'm sorry," but I never had the chance because even in the worst of times a child's words can lighten a father's heart. "Oh Daddy!" Jaymee bubbled. "Think how beautiful the bulls would look under the blue-light! Mirry and I sparkled like angels!"

It was a cold November day when Miracle's wandering wild cat tendencies began in earnest. Evening came and she didn't come in when we called.

"I'll bet the owls got her," said Becky.

"Uh, uuh!" Jaymee scowled at her sister. "She'll come

home. You'll see."

Then the phone rang. "Does your little kid have a white cat?" asked a hay buyer who'd picked up a ton of alfalfa just before noon. He lived sixty miles away.

"Yes," I said.

"I reckon it likes to ride in trucks," he continued. "Didn't know it was there till I got home. Musta curled up near the engine to keep warm while I was loadin' up." A muscle flicked in Bill's jaw as he reached for his hat and he and Jaymee disappeared into the darkness for the 120-mile round trip to bring Miracle home.

Before long, Miracle became a seasoned traveler like all wildcats. Although they might spend only a few months with us, familiar survivors returned again and again, some every year, others skipping a year or two. I felt a certain sadness because we had so hoped we could turn this wild cat into a domestic cat. Furthermore, we'd all become attached to this little white ghost of the night.

We cautioned buyers to check under the hoods and behind the seats before they left, but it soon became obvious Jaymee's little cat liked touring the world beyond Singing Valley. Although cars and trucks were a favorite mode of travel, she vanished more often on foot and was gone for days at a time. When she finally came home, Jaymee exclaimed, "She's filthy! Just like a dirty old wild cat," and gave her a bath.

"Maybe dirty's safer," I warned. "She blends with the desert." But Jaymee didn't want her to be dirty.

On Miracle's first birthday, owls were hatching, coyotes were whelping, and snakes were shedding their skins. I heard Scott yell from a horse corral. "Miracle! Get outta there!" And in the next breath, "Dad! Rattler!"

Bill grabbed a shovel from the pickup, and I dashed to the tack room for the anti-venom kit. The diamondback had struck a mare between the nostrils. The horse was staggering, pawing the ground, her eyes white-rimmed with panic. In minutes her head had swelled to the size of a rhinoceros' head. She couldn't breathe. During the agonizing hour that followed, I remember spotting Miracle under the manure spreader. She looked — strange. But the mare was our worry now. We had to save her.

Not until Bill had administered the antidote and thrust a four-foot plastic filter tube from our tropical fish tank up the mare's nose and down her throat so she could get some air, did Scott say, "If it hadn't been for Mirry, that flash of white, I wouldn't have seen this happen.

The cat was going bonkers over that snake, leaping around, jumping at those rattles like she wanted to play." He stopped and looked at me. "Mom. I think the snake got Miracle too."

I ran to the little cat. She lay motionless — eyes sealed, her head bigger than her body. Bill picked up the bottle of anti-venom serum. It was empty. "I'll try some cortisone," he murmured. "It's all we've got."

I carried the seemingly lifeless ball of white fluff onto the porch and laid her gently in her box. Two days later Miracle was still in a coma when we saw Jaymee press two fingers against the little cat's chest like she'd seen Bill do with a dying calf. "Mirry's going to be fine," she said in a choked voice. "I think I can feel her heart still beating."

Emotion flickered across Bill's face then and, though weary from a long day, he got up from the table and returned a few minutes later with his cattle stethoscope and knelt beside her. "Here, honey. Try this." He hung the stethoscope from Jaymee's ears. Then, holding the monitor in his big callused hand, he pressed it to the little cat's ribs right where the heart should be and watched the face of the child he loved. Suddenly her dark eyes brimmed and fastened on his. "Oh, Daddy," she cried, "I hear it! Now I know she's going to live!"

Miracle's recovery was slow, and we vowed when she got well we would never let her outside again, but good intentions don't always last, and as her strength returned, so did her nomadic dreams. Furthermore, doors open and close. Cats sneak out. If only her fur didn't signify prey.

Jaymee stopped bathing her. With so little rain, predators abounded on the ranch and we feared the inevitable. Sometimes Miracle disappeared for days or weeks at a time, only to return looking more independent, scuffed up and dustier than ever. By fall she was gone more than she was home. Was she in fact returning to her roots?

"She's starting to look more and more like a wild cat," Jaymee said when the little cat returned with her first scar, a diagonal wrinkle between her blue eyes. "I wonder what she eats?" Although we talked about desert menus — bugs, birds, lizards and rodents — Jaymee liked to think there were other ranchers and farmers who fed her the right things when she stopped by to "bum a meal," things like fresh cow's milk and cat chow.

Miracle was only two-and-a-half when she disappeared for the last time. Another year of drought, and predators had taken most of our domestic cats as well as those from the wild. Perhaps the owls were to blame. Or coyotes? Maybe the return of eagles from Mexico? We would never know because nature keeps her secrets. But cats, both wild and tame, had become as much a part of our ranch as the cattle, horses, chickens and wildlife. They'd found a place to call home. We missed them. Miracle most of all.

Although Jaymee would come to love many cats over the years, Miracle would always remain closest to her heart. We had all been victims of the little white cat's subtle magnetism. Even Bill — in his own way. Yet never in our wildest dreams did we realize that hours spent in play on the back porch and feed room had been mere rehearsals for perilous acts of survival she would need for the life she chose. The life of a wild cat.

One evening, three years after Miracle disappeared, Bill came in, his eyes bright with mischief. "Jaymee!" he called. "Come outside a minute! I gotta show you something." We all followed.

Camouflaged against the weathered-metal barn roof crouched a battered little cat. Its dusty fur was puckered with scars, its right ear pasted to its skull. But the left ear, though ripped and torn, betrayed a trace of calico.

"Mirry!" Jaymee whispered, her face glowing with excitement.

All of us shared Jaymee's joy, but I also felt concern because I was sure this was no longer the "Mirry" she'd loved years before. This was a battle-hardened wild cat. In her world there could be no room for memories of the little girl who'd held her and bathed her and cherished her quirky little ways. Jaymee had been shattered when Miracle disappeared for those three years. Would she be hurt even worse now when Miracle failed to recognize her?

Meanwhile, spellbound, we all watched as Miracle's eyes fixed on a small brown bird nearby.

"No, Mirry!" Jaymee screamed. "Don't kill it!"

The cat hesitated. Then shifting her gaze toward Jaymee's familiar voice, she eased down and leapt into Jaymee's outstretched arms. "I knew you'd come back!" Jaymee said. "I knew it!"

Except for occasional two-day trips, Miracle roamed no more. She ate cat food, left mice on the doorstep and seemed to settle down to domestic cat life until the morning Bill found her on the seat of his John Deere tractor. Her rugged little heart had simply stopped. She was only seven years old. "At least Mirry died at home,"

Jaymee said quietly, "with her family."

Yes, I thought, certain now in my own heart that even in the strangest of animal cultures, a child's love *can* overcome the ultimate call of the wild.

September 22, 1979

This weekend we went to a bull sale at John Wayne's 26-Bar Ranch near Casa Grande. The actor enjoyed being the person he really is for the day, talking about bulls, breeding and cattle prices with all the ranchers. But he never turned down an offer to stand with his hand on a young boy's shoulder so a mother could take a picture of "the Duke" and her son Although the sale was planned for fellow ranchers, fans' cars stretched for miles and there was food for everybody and anybody.

The major topic of conversation among the cattle buyers was purchasing shares in prize bulls. This meant no one got to bring the bull home to his ranch. Instead, he would receive a tank with 40 to 100 vials of semen stored in liquid nitrogen. Artificial insemination and embryo transplanting are becoming the rage. Ranchers, including Bill and Scott, have to go back to school to learn all about this scientific advancement, and like everything else in the ranching world, stories would be told about it..

Ranchers raising registered cattle, as we do, hope to have calf crops evenly divided; 50% bulls and 50% heifers. Unfortunately, Singing Valley Ranch always seems to get far more heifers than bull calves. Then two years ago, so the story goes, a Canadian rancher discovered that if he inseminated his cows so their heads faced west and their tails east during the procedure chances for bulls were 80% greater. Bill tried it (just for fun). And it worked. But only that first year. The following year he had 75% heifers again so there were lots of offers to help him turn his chute around.

LOVE ON THE WING

One unforgettable morning, while jouncing along twisting cattle trails and dirt roads on our Arizona Hereford ranch, we came across the mourning doves. Pegged out like clothespins along miles of sagging telephone wires, their sunlit feathers reflected rainbows in the early glow of dawn, but bead-bright eyes were riveted on our pickup load of grain.

"Dumbest birds on earth!" Bill grumbled as he pulled up beside the first of six eighteen-foot aluminum feed troughs.

"Why do you always call them dumb, Daddy?" Jaymee asked.

"Because doves are out to kill themselves before they even hatch." He struggled to light his pipe, a familiar sign he had more to say. "They fly into windowpanes and break their necks. They lean over too far and drown in stock tanks." He climbed from the truck and hauled an eighty-pound sack of grain onto his shoulder. "And they build nests with such big holes in the bottom they wouldn't hold a ping-pong ball, let alone an egg."

"Then how come there's so many?" Jaymee called as we watched him buck his way through the herd of milling cattle, rip open a sack and begin to pour. He never had time to answer.

Alerted by the clatter of grain, doves suddenly darkened the sky. We heard the surge of whistling wings, and the phantom rush of air as they swooped down in a frenzied quest for corn. Some lit on the cows' horns. Others blanketed their backs. But most silvered the earth like a restless sea around the stomping hooves of cattle.

Jaymee screamed, "Daddy! That cow's standing on a dove's wing!"

Bill tossed the empty feed sack into the back of the pickup and hurried toward the cow. "Dumb bird," he muttered as he twisted the cow's tail till she shifted her weight. The dove was free, but one wing lay on the ground, severed from its body at the shoulder.

I don't know how long we watched the pathetic creature flap its remaining wing and spin in useless circles as though winding itself into the ground. At last it tipped forward, buried its beak in the dirt, and mercifully lay still.

Thank God! I thought, torn between scrambled emotions of sadness and relief. It's dead. After all, there was nothing we could do for a bird with only one wing.

Bill nudged the dove with the toe of his boot. Horrified, we watched it flip onto its back, wild-eyed with pain. Jaymee's small hands flew to her lips. "Oh, no!" she cried. "It's still alive! Daddy, do something!"

Bill leaned down and wrapped the tiny, broken creature in his red handkerchief and handed it to Jaymee. "Here, honey," he said, "you'll have to hold it till we get home."

"But it's going to die!" I heard the tremor of fear in her voice.

"I don't think so," he said. "They're even—" I caught his eye and defied him to say "too dumb to die."

"What are we going to do with it, Mama?" Jaymee's brow was creased with worry. Only eight years old, she loved small animals and was forever rescuing soft, fluffy kittens, baby rabbits, and ground squirrels. But this was different. This was a bird. Furthermore, it was grotesquely wounded.

"We'll put it in a box, give it water and grain." I stopped right there, knowing too well the rest was up to God.

Sorrow clouded Jaymee's small face. "But if it lives, it won't ever be able to fly again, and it'll have to live in a cage — forever."

"Lots of birds do," I said.

"But those are canaries and parakeets . . . and they're pretty." Then in a whisper she added, " and they're smart."

On our way back to the house, Jaymee sat quietly between us holding the young dove in her lap. Deep in thoughts of her own, she stroked its tiny head with two fingers until she walked into the kitchen where Becky, her ten-year-old sister, was eating breakfast. She showed her the bird. "A cow chopped off its wing," she told her.

Becky wrinkled her nose. Then later, after putting the bird in a shoe box filled with dried grass and setting the box and bird near the wood stove for warmth, Becky asked, "What are you going to name it?"

"Olive," Jaymee said.

"Olive! That's an awful name. Why Olive?"

"Because Noah's dove flew all the way back to the ark with an olive branch . . . and that wasn't so dumb."

While the girls were in school, I listened for sounds of life from the box and repeatedly peeked inside at the tiny gray ghostlike creature hiding in the dark, head drooped, rainbows gone. In the barn I found a jar of antibiotic salve. "For Olive," I said to Bill, wishing I could have slipped by unseen.

He shrugged.

"Well, it's worth a try," I insisted, hurrying back to the house. There I lathered the hideous wound with the medicine and asked myself, Why am I doing this? More to the point, I wondered why nature hadn't simply claimed the life of this pitiful creature. How could this bird live with only one wing? Poor little thing. Certain it was suffering, convinced it would die, I closed the lid. We'd done everything we could.

The next morning, we heard a stirring in the box. "Olive's eating!" Jaymee announced. Then, with absolute conviction, she added, "and she's a girl."

"How can you tell?" Becky asked.

"Boys have blue and purple feathers on their heads. Olive's just plain gray — and sometimes pink."

We kept the little bird near the stove in a large wire-mesh cage prepared with seeds, leaves and twigs. In the sudden shock of light and space, Olive sensed freedom and again tried to fly. She flapped her one wing, repeatedly hurling herself against the wire-mesh squares, waffing her breast feathers and falling over backward. It hurt to watch her try.

In time the wing fluttered slower and slower till

finally it stopped altogether. From then on, Olive wandered around the cage sort of off-kilter, like half a bird, barely existing yet taking the time to preen and rearrange her feathers as though trying to draw a cape over the gaping hole. When evening came, she curled her pink claws around a small manzanita limb we'd wedged in the bottom of the cage in one corner. There she perched in a trancelike state, dreaming of life in the sky, I supposed, a life put on hold, until . . .

Early one morning, Jaymee was cleaning the cage. "Olive laid an egg!" she squealed. "Come look!" Resembling an elliptical, oversized pearl, the egg rolled around like a magic thing between a few twigs and leaves in Olive's favorite corner of the cage. "But why didn't she build a nest?" Jaymee asked.

"Just like in the wild," Bill said, "too lazy to build a decent nest. They either lay their eggs in other birds' nests or slap three twigs together and call it home."

He was right. I, too, had seen doves' nests: flimsy little platforms, tossed at random among the mesquite and manzanita bushes, spanned weak boughs or remnant nests of other birds. Some were precariously balanced on knots of mistletoe. Most were within easy reach of predators: the bobcat, raccoon and coyote. I'd walked often beneath branches to view the eggs from below, or discovered the empty, broken shells at my feet after they'd fallen through. Yet these birds kept right on laying in the same miserable nests.

Now here was Olive, caged, piteously wounded, soon laying an egg almost every day. For Jaymee, this was magic. But I had to question the little bird's efforts. Why was this happening? Without a mate, the eggs would be infertile. But Jaymee was a child, and children make plans. Instead of worrying about why, she accepted the miracle with her whole heart and began collecting the eggs in a teacup.

At first Bill didn't pay much attention to the dove. He had cattle, horses and fields to care for. But then one Sunday, when he noticed Jaymee's cup was full, he made plans of his own. Out in his workshop he built a wooden eggbox for her with a clear plastic lid revealing forty two-inch cubicles padded with black velvet inside. "It's a treasure chest," he told her, "with a special place for each little egg." When he handed her the key to the tiny brass padlock, he added, "You can keep them safe forever." She hugged him.

By now Olive was becoming very tame. No longer spooked by human hands, she tottered around the cage with anticipation. At the sight of Jaymee, she cooed softly and pecked seeds or morsels of apple from her palm. And when Jaymee took her out of the cage to carry her around on her finger, the little dove no longer tried to fly. Instead she perched, seemingly content, and shared an ice cream cone till it was time to go back in the cage — and lay another egg.

Like all creatures wild and tame, Olive responded to love and care with growing trust. She looked forward to her daily dust bath in the metal cake pan filled with sand, and she especially enjoyed her shower, a gentle misting of water from a spray bottle, after which she cleaned her feathers vigorously. We liked to think she was happy. But our crippled dove's longing for her own kind and a life she'd left behind showed when we moved her cage to the glassed-in porch where she could look out at the cobalt sky and sun-drenched fields of green alfalfa. Occasionally another dove would sail by and Olive's wing would quiver and her little gray head would bob anxiously, begging to be noticed.

Incredibly, the egg laying continued. Sixteen! Seventeen! Eighteen! How much longer can this go on? I wondered.

Bill shared our concern with a gruff "The bird's gonna lay herself to death." At least he didn't say "dumb," I thought. Recently I'd caught him putting small logs in the cattle troughs. "Rafts," he'd said when I inquired, "so the doves can climb out when they fall in." Was he starting to care just a little bit? Or had he always, in his own way?

When the nineteenth egg arrived, so did the first storm out of Mexico. Fearsome winds and stinging sands ripped birds' nests from the trees, dashing eggs and the newly hatched to the ground. The girls spent the morning burying dead newborns before the barn cats got them, and Jaymee gathered many different kinds of wild bird eggs, miraculously unbroken, and put them in her treasure chest. Most had tinted shells, rainbow colors, I thought, displayed like precious jewels among pearls on velvet black.

One storm often follows another in Arizona, so I wasn't surprised when the second roared through and Jaymee dashed into the kitchen cupping a naked-pink, open-beaked baby bird in her hands. "It's hungry!" she cried. "Maybe Olive can be its mama."

I wasn't so sure, but Jaymee hurriedly named the newborn "Pinky." With an eyedropper we squeezed chick-mash mixed with warm water into the orphan's yawning yellow mouth and debated bestowing such a helpless gift on our fragile dove.

What will she do? I wondered. Then I realized, What did it matter? We didn't know how to keep the hours-old creature the right temperature at night anyway. Only a mother bird could do that. My broody hen hatched and raised baby ducks, guinea hens, pheasants and quail along with her own chicks. So why couldn't a dove raise a stranger too? Besides, if it worked, life in a cage wouldn't be so lonesome for Olive.

I asked Bill what he thought. "She'll probably think he's dinner," he said.

Jaymee's eyes widened. "Oh, Daddy," she scolded. "Olive's smarter than that. We've got to try!"

"We'll fix up a nice nest first," I said, "a good sturdy one like a dove should make, soft and deep so the baby won't fall out." The girls found a storm-damaged nest and lined it with horse hair and plenty of chicken feathers for added softness. I worried the feathers might have an alien scent that Olive wouldn't appreciate, but since doves frequently feasted side by side with my chickens, I decided she wouldn't mind. Also, since Pinky was already a scented bouquet of human hands and chicken mash, and Olive was accustomed to both, we laid the newborn in the nest with one egg of her own at his side.

"Maybe that will help her think the baby is really hers," Jaymee said, and placed the nest inside the cage.

During the night I awoke to strange sounds, living reminders that wild birds belong outdoors — not in my kitchen. Expecting the worst, I reached for my flashlight, not wanting to awaken Bill, and hurried to the scene. The nest was destroyed. At first I couldn't see any birds at all. Then, in that favorite corner where eggs were laid, one of nature's miracles unfolded like a flower bud in the beam of my light. On three small twigs, bright eyes aglow with joy, nested Olive — with Pinky cradled under her only wing.

The egg laying ceased. Pinky had a mother. Proud and protective, Olive chirped anxiously when we took him out for feeding countless times a day. When we put him back in Olive's nest, with a little dry grass tucked around and under him so he wouldn't tip over, she paced back and forth till she was certain he wasn't leaving again. Then she examined him thoroughly, picking and tweaking him as though trying to weave their lives together. It was clear to see she loved him.

Pinky thrived. Pink skin one day, milkweed-down the next. Finally, feathers appeared on stubby wings, then everywhere. A delicate tapestry of silver-white and black, the fledgling soon needed a far more fitting name. When the short, hooked beak was topped by a tiny black-bandit mask, our bird book dubbed him a loggerhead shrike, lover of wetlands and rarely seen on our ranch after several years of drought. Jaymee renamed him Bandit.

Soon Bandit was perching on Jaymee's finger just like his mama did. Teetering on tiny black claws, he gobbled down spaghetti, bologna and pepperoni sliced into slender worm-like strips. As more feathers grew, his gourmet palate expanded to include moths, bugs and any insect Jaymee could pick up with eyebrow tweezers. His passion was flies, but they had to be alive.

Flies are a part of ranch and farm life, and a door rarely opened without a herd of these miserable pests stampeding in. Unable to get out, they'd sizzle up and down window panes and fall on the sills, exhausted. Then Jaymee grabbed them by one leg with the tweezers, and fed them still buzzing to Bandit, while Olive waited patiently for her serving on the bottom of the cage.

The morning we'd been dreading came when Bandit discovered he had wings. We found him clinging upsidedown to the top of the cage. Unable to figure out how to let go, he chatted, and fluttered his wings eagerly, while Olive cringed in her corner, feathers frazzled.

"You're going to have to let him go," Bill told Jaymee. "He's scaring the heck out of the poor dove."

"But he needs to practice flying first," she argued, removing Bandit from the cage and perching him on her finger. Instantly, the young shrike took a test flight. He shot up and positioned himself on the wagonwheel chandelier, took stock of his surroundings and shuttled awkwardly to the bullhorn hat rack, from there to the toaster. By now Olive was chirping with alarm.

"Jaymee. You've got to put him outside," Bill said. "I don't want feathers in my coffee."

"But the cats'll get him!"

"He has to learn," he responded. Outside we placed Bandit in a cottonwood tree so he could practice flying. We watched him flit from branch to branch and grabbed him twice when he landed on the ground. He learned fast. Too fast. The moment we tried to step inside, he zipped past us through the doorway and greeted us from the chandelier. Then he heard Olive and dived to the top of the cage where she watched him from below, her wing vibrating with memory.

"She wants to go with him," Jaymee said sadly.

And he doesn't understand why she can't come, I

thought.

Bandit remained housebound. Every time we took him outside, he'd perch for an hour on the milk separator right by the front door, mask cocked, wings ready, waiting patiently for someone to go through the door so he could sneak back in.

Night came. We knew he'd never survive with so many barn cats on the prowl. Furthermore, spring rains had lured many birds back to the lands by the White River draw. Perhaps the shrikes would return? Until he was ready to be on his own, we had to keep him safe, so we rigged up a temporary nighttime cage near Olive's. She seemed pleased.

Bandit grew increasingly adept at flying and was soon darting in and out of the front door at will, eager to remain part of the only home he knew. I warned Bill and everybody else, "Be careful when you come in for lunch. Our little shrike is going to sneak in, and he might get hurt if the door shuts too quickly."

As fate would have it, Bill was the one who forgot. Worse still, it was he who had put the heavy-duty spring on the door so it would snap shut faster and not let so many flies into the house. When he saw the little bird spiral over his head and land on the rug at his feet, his first words were, "I guess I had other things on my mind besides holding a door open for a bird." Then his voice dropped, and I could tell something was struggling within him. "I never saw the poor thing at all . . . till it was lying in front of me."

For the second time that year I watched him lean over to pick up a wounded bird. They are so delicate, and I knew he felt bad. Bandit was gasping, but the tiny needle-clawed feet gripped Bill's callused palm. Reassured, Bill said, "Maybe he just got the wind knocked out of him." He handed the stunned creature to me to put back in its cage, right beside Olive's.

The next day, Bandit seemed cheerful enough but ruffled at being caged. We let him out. No longer the wing-testing, house-crashing maniac of previous flights, he flitted quite professionally among barn roofs, scattered trees and barbed-wire fences. Our little shrike had grown up, and gradually he flew farther away. Easy to spot in his flashing white and black and silver, wingbeats too fast to count, we watched him leave for the river. That was the last we saw of him.

Later in the summer, the girls were busy getting their projects ready for the Cochise County Fair only ten days away. Becky planned to show her horse, and Jaymee busied herself grooming her rabbits for the 4-H competitions. The egg chest had been set aside, perhaps for the following year, when suddenly Jaymee said, "Maybe I should show Olive and her eggs in the wildlife division too."

"But Olive's been sick," I reminded her. Indeed, after Bandit's departure the little mourning dove had begun sleeping most of the day. Eyes half closed, she perched unnaturally fluffed on her manzanita limb. The only sign she showed of interest in life came with the early dawn: a plaintive "Oooh-ah-hoo-hoo-hoo," like the sorrowful cry of a lost soul in the desert, seeking comfort. Then she started molting.

Clearly unwell, she soon didn't seem to care where she roosted. Often she simply crouched uncomfortably over a few stray twigs and leaves. We tried to cheer her through her long dark hours of sadness by adding sugar to her water and a nightlight to her cage. I played happy songs on the radio. Nothing worked. When she stopped taking dust baths altogether and dripped resentfully in a pool of water after misting, I was afraid she was going to die.

Then Bill returned from the feed store in Tucson with a truckload of cattle feed — and one small box that read Special Diet for Indisposed Canaries. "I just happened to walk through the small pet section," he said, looking a little sheepish. "A bird's a bird, but I thought maybe a couple of vitamins might help Olive." To our surprise, she seemed to perk up.

Jaymee added the cost of her daddy's purchase to her list of eggs, dates laid, and in miscellaneous dove project expenses added to her 4-H journal. She even entered a paragraph about Olive's baby, Bandit, and facts she had learned from books about doves. "Unlike most birds," she wrote, "doves will keep right on laying when their eggs slip through flimsy nests or are stolen by predators." And finally, "Doves have been known to lay more than one clutch (nest of eggs) at a time, incubate a second and even a third batch while raising a lucky survivor from the first."

Meanwhile, Becky weighed Jaymee's idea about displaying her treasure chest, and she did an egg count for her sister. "You only have thirty-one, Jaymee. That leaves nine empty holes, so the project isn't complete. You'll have to wait till next year when birds start laying again."

I felt a strange sense of relief because Olive had never fully recovered from her sadness, despite the vitamins. She'd become frail, dusty looking, almost spectral. If she were around strange animals and surroundings at the fair, I feared she would pick up an infection. At home she'd be safe. Then, the following morning, she laid another egg.

Hope lit Jaymee's eyes. She put the egg in her treasure chest—number thirty-two. "Only eight more to go," she said happily and dashed off to catch every live fly she could find for Olive.

During the short week that followed, Olive rallied with six more eggs. Then three days before the fair, and two more eggs to go, our weary little dove huddled on her manzanita limb for the last time. We found her in the morning, motionless, like a tiny piece of driftwood washed up on desert sands.

"Do you think Olive was happy locked in a cage?" Jaymee asked her daddy as he wrapped the little one-winged dove in his red handkerchief, just as he'd done only a few short months ago.

"Why . . . of course she was," he answered awkwardly.

"How do you know for sure?"

He looked over Jaymee's head at me as though grasping for thoughts, trying to make sense out of the life of a bird. Then, in a blur of words that a man would never say except to a child, he stumbled ahead. "You took care of her. You fed her and . . . and gave her showers . . . and a baby . . . and told her how smart she was." He paused for a long moment. "And you know, she was smart . . . because out of all those things you did for her, she knew how much you loved her."

"And she gave me her eggs because she loved me too?"

"Her treasures," he said. "All that she had." He watched his youngest child gather two small handfuls of pale pink and gray feathers and fill the empty velvet nests before she turned the key.

"I'm going to show my egg collection anyway, Daddy," she murmured.

He smiled and hugged her. "I'll bet you win the blue ribbon."

And she did.

November 10, 1981

Oh so many horses! To think it all began with one Appaloosa gelding named Tonka. Becky loved him and rode in all the 4-H shows. Then Jaymee thought she wanted a horse too. From there our equine population has grown to fields and corrals full of brood mares and assorted young geldings and fillies — and five stallions waiting in corrals — impatiently. These horses are not all ours. Most are boarders, which include all breeds from paints to thoroughbreds. Scott does all the breaking, training and handling the studs, while Bill soothes the mares.

With all the coming and going of mares to get in foal we average eighty head at one time. Multiply eighty times four hooves that need trimming or shoeing every six weeks and that's 320 "feet. This calls for a full-time horseshoer.

Henry Marble is our farrier. There isn't a horse he can't shoe no matter how "loco" the animal is. He can break a bronc in less than an hour. Causing no pain, he uses a few ropes and gentle words to make a horse lie down, stop kicking, get up and load into a trailer, and he urges the animal to eat grain from his hand as reward. Henry is also a shop teacher at Benson High School and an elder in the Mormon Church of Elfrida. He lost his job when he taught the proper care, respect, and handling of guns.

But Henry has many other remarkable talents. He can

cure anything from head colds, headaches, to dislocated joints with a simple, quick neck adjustment. Bill says he is a "self-appointed" chiropractor.

This morning, a green-broke horse tossed a hired hand into a ditch. Several of the man's vertebrae were knocked out of alignment. The poor guy tilted like a teapot. Henry told him to "quit whimpering," made him hang upside down by his knees from the bars in a stallion pen, then cranked his neck. The man was cured. However, the neck-cranking sound almost undid me. But who am I to question? It wasn't my neck. It worked.

Henry makes saddle, bridles . . . and he pulls teeth too!

OUR HORSE OF A DIFFERENT COLOR

"When it comes to horses, what you want and what you get are often two different things." Bill, weary from building a new hay barn, kept up his warning to me even as he fell asleep that night.

But I am a dreamer, and foaling season is a time for dreams. After years of raising Hereford cattle on our Arizona ranch, we'd just become Appaloosa breeders, and I was dreaming of precious foals, blue ribbons and eager buyers.

That first year, the dazzling hair-coats of nine little Appaloosas had already transformed our pastures into a landscape of color. Their tiny faces were bright with stars and blazes, their rumps glittering with patches and spots splashed over them like suds.

Bill and I were sure our tenth foal of the year, due before dawn, would be the most colorful of all. Its father was a white stud with chestnut spots over more than half his body and a multicolored tail that touched the ground. The mother was covered with thousands of penny-sized copper dots. I already had a name for their unborn treasure: Starburst.

Normally, I would have been awaiting this new arrival in our freezing corral, numb fingers clutching a flashlight. But tonight was different. Bill had bought me a closed-circuit TV, which he set up on my side of the bed. That way, I could watch the monitor in comfort and observe the mare's progress. Then when she reached her last stage of labor, if help was needed, I'd rush to her side.

Now, on the screen, I could see the spotted mare's hide glistening with sweat. White-rimmed eyes betrayed her anxiety, and dust devils swirled like headless ghosts in the wake of her pacing hooves. Suddenly she stopped cold. Nostrils wide, ears twitching back and forth, she listened for dangers in the night. It'll be a while yet until she foals, I thought, and I dozed off.

I awoke with a jolt. Three hours had passed. A glance at the monitor revealed the mare flat out on her side, steam rising from her body in the frosty air. The birth was over. But where was her foal? I sat up fast, studying the screen and searching the fuzzy shadows and distant corners of the corral. It was gone.

"Bill! Wake up!" I shook him hard. "Something stole the baby!"

Wild dogs, hungry coyotes and bobcats raided my imagination. I was the one who walked the night when we had calves or foals being born, and I remembered catching a raccoon slaughtering my chickens in the moonlight. I remembered a bobcat, daggers glinting from his eyes, as he slithered across the roof of our rabbit hutch. One midnight, I'd even seen a bear lumbering past our mailbox.

Moments later, after leaping into my jeans and sneakers and grabbing a jacket, I was on my knees in the dimly lit corral, stroking the mare's neck. "Where's your baby, Mama?" I called, almost crying in panic. "Where'd it go?"

Suddenly a plaintive whinny rose from behind the water trough. Then I saw a face pop out of the shadows — thin, long, dark, ugly. The ears hung like charred pot holders from a rusty hook. Right away, I realized why I hadn't seen this newborn on my TV. No colorful spots. No blazing coat. The foal was brown as dirt.

"I don't believe it," I said, as Bill crouched down beside me for a closer look. "There's not a single white hair on her." We saw more unwanted traits: a bulging forehead, a hideous, sloping Roman nose, and a nearly hairless bobtail.

"She's a real throwback," Bill said, standing up. I

knew we were both thinking the same thing. This filly would be just another mouth to feed. She'd never sell. After all, who wants an Appaloosa without color?

By now the spotted mare was on her feet, eyeing this trembling little stranger with contempt. The foal staggered toward her and tried to nurse. The mare wheeled and kicked, knocking the baby to the ground in a scrambled heap. It cried out with fear and surprise.

"Whoa, Mama!" Bill shouted. "Stop that!" He lifted the foal back on her feet. "I'll get the mare some hay," he said. "She needs to be by herself." I knew he was right. Nature would take care of bonding if we left them alone. But after Bill tossed some alfalfa on the ground, hoping to quiet the mare, the filly tried to nurse again. This time the kick was so violent it sent the baby skidding under the fence.

"Oh, Bill," I pleaded, wrapping my arms around the shivering foal, "help me stand her up — just one more time." Once she was on her feet, I stayed with her a minute, steadying her. "You'll be okay, little one," I murmured. "Just keep on trying." I hated to leave but knew it was best.

The next morning, when Scott arrived for work and saw our newest addition, he minced no words. "What are we going to do with that ugly thing?" he asked.

By now, the baby had nursed, but it looked like all the nourishment had gone to her ears. They stood straight up in the air. "She looks just like a mule," Scott said. "Who's going to want her?"

Our younger girls, Becky and Jaymee, now fifteen and twelve, had questions of their own. "How will anyone know she's an Appaloosa?" Becky asked. "Are there spots under the fur?"

"No," I told her, "she's what's called a 'solid.' That means no breed characteristics at all. But she's still an Appy inside."

That's when Jaymee came up with the glorious wisdom of a twelve-year-old. "That means she's got spots on her heart."

Who knows, I wondered. Maybe she does.

From the beginning, the homely filly seemed to sense she was different. Visitors rarely looked at her, and if they did we found ourselves saying, "Oh, we're just boarding the mother." We didn't want anyone to know our beautiful stallion had sired this ugly foal. After all, mare owners seeking an Appaloosa stud want to be convinced he produces only quality babies with small heads, straight legs, neat little ears, long flowing tails and — above all—a coat of many colors.

When the filly was two weeks old, we turned her and her mother out to pasture with the herd. Being the newcomer, she was afraid to romp with the other foals because their mothers bared their teeth at her. Worse still, her own mother now seemed to sense her offspring needed all the protection she could get. So she angrily charged any horse that came within fifteen feet of her little one. Even if another foal ventured too close, the mother lashed out with a vicious snap. Little by little our bobtailed filly learned the world was a place to fear.

Before long, I started noticing something else — she relished human company. She and her mother were first at the gate at feeding time and, when I scratched her neck and shoulders, her eyelids closed in contentment. Soon she was nuzzling my jacket, running her lips over my shirt, chewing my buttons off and even opening the gate to follow me so she could rub her head on my hip.

"Mom's got herself another lame duck," I overheard Scott say to his dad one day.

Bill sighed. "Oh, God. What is it this time?"

"That jugheaded filly. What else?"

Unfortunately, her appetite was huge. And the bigger

she got, the uglier she got. Where will we ever find a home for her? I wondered.

One day a man bought a beautiful two-year-old "leopard" gelding from us for a circus. He spied the brown bobtailed filly. "That's not an Appaloosa, is it?" he asked. "Looks like a donkey."

Since he was looking for circus horses, I snatched at the opportunity. "You'd be surprised," I said. "That filly knows more tricks than a short-order cook. She can take a handkerchief out of my pocket and Rolaids out of Bill's. She can crawl under fences, climb into water troughs, turn on spigots."

"Reg'lar little devil, huh?" he said.

"No, not really. As a matter of fact, I named her 'Angel!'"

He chuckled. "Well, it's eye-catchin' color we need at the Big Top," he told me. "Folks like spotted horses best."

I knew he was right, but as his truck and trailer rattled down the dirt road, I pictured our homely filly jumping through flaming hoops with white poodles in pink tutus clinging to her back. Why couldn't a plain brown horse do the same thing? I wondered.

As time passed, Angel, as we now called her, invented new tricks. Her favorite was opening gates to get food on the opposite side. "She's a regular Houdini," Bill marveled.

"She's a regular pain," said Scott, who always had to catch her.

"Maybe two chains and double clips'll work better than one," I suggested. It made no difference. Angel's hunger for anything edible on the other side of the fence persisted, and the jingle-jangle of horse teeth against metal chains on corral gates never stopped as she honed her skills.

With Angel's huge appetite, I tried giving her an extra flake of hay before bed. Her affection for me grew. Unfortunately, so did her appetite. One morning Scott found her in the hay barn, whinnying a greeting. Broken bales littered the floor. Her sides bulged. Scott was disgusted.

"You've got to be more patient and give her some attention, Scott," I told him. "You spend all your time grooming and training the other yearlings. You never touch Angel except to yell at her."

"Who has time to work with a jughead?" he grumbled. "Besides, Dad said we're taking her to auction."

"What! And sell her for dog food?"

I corralled Bill. "Let her grow up on the ranch," I begged. "Then Scott can saddle-break her when she's two. With her sweet nature she'll be worth something to someone by then."

"I guess one more horse won't hurt for the time being," he said. "We'll put her down on the east pasture. There's not much grazing there, but . . ." He was keeping his options open. Still, Angel was safe — for now.

Two weeks later she was at the front door eating dry dog food from our watchdog's bowl. She'd slipped the chain off the pasture gate and let herself out — plus ten other horses as well. By the time Scott and Bill had rounded them up, I could see that Bill's patience was wearing thin. He turned to the girls. "You two, give her some attention. School's out now. Maybe you can even make her pretty."

That summer, they groomed her, bathed her — and looked for spots. They even rubbed mayonnaise and Swedish hair-grow into the stubbly mane and tail. This folk remedy worked with some horses, but not with Angel. When they tried to brush her teeth, she simply ate the toothbrush. That was on top of all the cantaloupes and watermelons they fed her. She ate everything. Angel loved all the attention and, perhaps to show it, she even stopped opening gates.

Then school started and Angel lost her playmates. Scott came into the kitchen one morning, fuming. "That filly's gotta go, Mom" he said. "She got into the tack room last night, pulled bridles off the hooks, knocked saddles on the floor, chewed up a tube of toothpaste the girls left on the sink. She's gonna stay in that east pasture if we have to build a wall around it."

Fortunately, the rains came. The grass grew. Angel stayed in without a wall and now she got fat as a buffalo — and her assortment of tricks grew. When Bill or Scott drove to the field to check on the herd, she'd chew the sideview mirrors off the truck, eat the rubber off the windshield wipers, or bend the aerial. If they left a window open, she'd poke her head inside, snatch a rag, wrench, glove or notebook off the front seat, and run away with it.

Surprisingly, Bill began forgiving Angel's pranks. In fact, soon we found ourselves looking forward to her best stunt of all. When an Appaloosa buyer would arrive, Angel would come at a gallop, slide to a stop about thirty feet away and back up to have her rump scratched. "We have our own circus right here," Bill told buyers. By now, a small smile was even showing through Scott's thick mustache.

The seasons rolled by. Scorching sun brought rain — and flies by the millions. One day, when Angel was two-and-a-half, I saw Scott leading her to the barn. Her rump was raw, bleeding and crawling with maggots from the hopeless thwacking of her hairless bobtail. "She gets no protection at all from that stupid tail," Scott told me as he treated Angel with antibiotics. "I'm gonna make her a new one." That's when I realized Scott's feelings for the horse were starting to change.

I smiled as he cut and twisted two dozen strands of bright yellow baling-twine into a long string mop and fastened it with adhesive wrap around her bandaged tail. "There," he patted her and stepped back to admire his handiwork, "she looks almost like a normal horse."

When Angel recovered, Scott decided to break her for riding. Bill and I sat on the corral fence as he put the saddle on. Angel humped her back. "We're going to have a rodeo here!" I whispered. But as Scott tightened the cinch around her plump middle, she didn't try to lie down and roll on the ground as some young horses do. She simply waited. When he climbed aboard and applied gentle pressure with his knees, the willing heart of the Appaloosa showed. He ordered her forward, and she responded as though she'd been ridden for years.

I reached up and scratched her bulging forehead. "Some day she's going to make a terrific trail-riding horse," I said, taking a moment to admire her tail. Every new shipment of baling twine came in different colors, red, orange, yellow, black. Today her tail was blue.

Scott seemed to know what I was thinking. "Blue's for winners, Mom," he said. "With a temperament like this, someone could even play polo off her. Or she could be a great kid's horse."

Now, even Scott was having a few dreams of his own for our plain brown Appaloosa with the funny colored tail.

Angel was soon helping Scott train young foals. Riding her, Scott would clip one end of a rope to a yearling's halter and wrap the other end around the saddlehorn. Angel would then pull, even drag, the younger horse along, but always with care.

At foaling time, she whinnied to the newborns as though each one were her own. "We ought to breed her," I said to Bill. "She's four. With her capacity to love, imagine what a good mother she'd make."

"Hey. That's not such a bad idea. People often buy

bred mares," he said. "Maybe we'd find a home for her." Suddenly I saw Scott frowning. Could he really care? I wondered.

For the first nine months of Angel's pregnancy, Scott kept her busy exercising yearlings. For once, she seemed to forget about escaping from her corral. Also, winter offered only dry, parched fields so the temptation to get out was gone until a heavy rain came, and our fields burst to life. She was getting closer to her due-date, and I tried not to hear the jingle of a chain because in my heart I knew Angel would once more start slipping through the gates in quest of greener pastures.

One morning we awoke to an unseasonable cold snap. I was starting breakfast when Scott opened the kitchen door, his hazel eyes looming dark beneath the broad-brimmed Stetson. "It's Angel, Mom," he said. "You better come. She got out of the corral last night."

Trying to hold back my fears, I followed him to his pickup. "She's had her foal somewhere," he said, "but Dad and I couldn't find it. She's . . . dying." I could hear the catch in his throat. He never got this close to animals. "Ate too much new grass, or maybe a poisonous weed." Suddenly his voice broke. "She's halfway between my house and here. Looks like she was trying . . . to make it home."

I scarcely heard him as unbidden memories rolled through my mind: the jingling of a security clasp, the rattle of chain, the creak of an old wooden gate being swung open. And now, last night, silhouetted against the rising moon, nostrils wide, testing secrets in the wind, our horse that nobody wanted had escaped for the last time.

When we got to Angel, Bill was crouched beside her, his boots sinking into the mud. "There's nothing we can do," he said, nodding toward the lush green fields, an easy reach for a hungry horse through the barbed wire. "Too much fresh alfalfa can be a killer."

I pulled Angel's huge head onto my lap and stroked the worn softness that the halter had left behind her too-big ears — those same ears that had made me think of charred pot holders when I found our dirt-brown filly hidden behind the water trough four years before.

Tears welled in Scott's eyes as he knelt beside me. "Best damned mare we ever had, Mom," he murmured.

Angel, I pleaded. *Please don't go!* But I felt our mare with all those "spots on her heart" slipping away. Choking back my grief, I ran my hand down the gentle darkness of her beautiful warm brown fur and listened to the heavy, labored breathing. The long legs strained, and her neck arched desperately backward, seeking one last breath of air. She shuddered. I looked into eyes that could no longer see. Angel was gone.

Then in a cloud of numbness, I heard Scott call out only a few yards away — disbelief in his voice. "Mom . . . Mom! Here's the foal. I found the foal!"

Deep in the sweet-smelling grasses where Angel had hidden him lay the foal of our dreams. A single spot brightened his tiny face, and a scattering of stars spangled his back and hips. A pure, radiant Appaloosa. Our horse of many colors. "Starburst," I whispered.

But somehow, all that color didn't matter any more. As his mother had taught us so many times over: It's not what's on the outside that counts. It's what lies deep in the heart. That's where Angel's spots and beauty were. It's that way with all animals — and it's that way with people too.

April 11, 1981

I love cows, but they have five stomachs, which can cause a lot of trouble. When they get a stomach ache, they can't throw up, so they blow up, instead, and die. This is called "bloat." Bill had to stab three cows in the side the other morning to let the air out in time to save them. They had eaten frost-covered alfalfa that was thawing in the morning sun, which gave them nitrite poisoning, so they bloated.

This morning Bill found another dead cow. This time, Doc White came out to do an autopsy. I watched. The first of the five stomachs was full of scraps of barbed wire, old staples, brass tacks and nails. "Just as I suspected," Doc said. "Hardware disease."

It seems that cattle love to chew on metal and swallow it. On windy ranches like ours, nails and staples ripped from roofs, fences and old barns can be found in every pasture, as well as all over the roads. With our all-terrain three-wheel motorcycles, we drag eighteen-inch magnets around the corrals and barnyards to pick up all the metal so we don't get so many flat tires.

Next week we are going to slip magnets into each cow's first stomach through a long plastic tube. Doc says instead of screws, rivets and lids from tin cans rupturing the stomach then piercing the heart, the metal objects will cling to the magnets and stay in the bottom of that first stomach and the cows can live a normal life. I hope it works.

THE BLOOMING OF TIGER LILY

We chose to raise Herefords at Singing Valley Ranch, beautiful white-faced beef cattle. Knowing that one day they would be sent to market, Bill always warned: "Don't ever get emotionally attached to a cow."

"Me?" I laughed and hugged him. "How would I ever have time for a cow with you and six children to love and take care of — and plenty of pets?"

But one Monday morning after chores, Bill came in for breakfast, an odd grin on his face. "Wait till you see what walked in last night," he said. "A stray calf — no mama, and no one's been looking for her."

That meant only one thing to me. Nobody wanted her. When Bill finished eating, I filled a bottle with calf suckle and hurried to the barns, guided to the right corral by the most heart-rending cry. A vision flashed across my mind — a curly, fluffy, adorable little calf, just like the rest of our Hereford babies. I couldn't wait.

I opened the corral gate. There, leaning against the fence on the far side, its head hanging to the ground, stood the ugliest, most rail-bodied, bandy-legged heifer calf I'd ever seen. She was sick, filthy, cut and bleeding, her long white face a haunting reminder of a skull bleached for years on the Arizona desert. Her bowed ribs stuck out like jail bars, threatening to split the dehydrated skin stretched over them. And her chapped nose bristled with cactus quills, infection and flies.

"I've got some penicillin and vitamins to give her," Bill said, coming up behind me. "Let's doctor her first, then we'll try the bottle." He handed me two hypodermic syringes and, crouching down, gripped the baby in his strong arms while I removed the cactus quills and plunged the needles into her thighs, hoping I wouldn't hit bone. The poor little calf never flinched.

"Good girl," I murmured and, still kneeling, I stroked the scrawny neck, put Vaseline on her nose and looked into the soft brown eyes sunken so deeply into their sockets. I could tell she was terrified, and something tore at my heart.

Bill misread my hesitation. "Don't worry," he said. "I'll take her to auction on Friday. But can you bottle her till then? Looks like she's part dairy. Holstein maybe. Somebody might want her."

At least she won't go for veal, I thought. Because we'd given her an antibiotic, she couldn't be butchered for sixty days. Once again I was glad we raised purebred cattle for breeding, which, in my roundabout thinking, dimmed the ultimate purpose of raising "good beef."

"Hurry up. Let's feed her," Bill said. "My knees are killing me."

I pushed the four-inch nipple into the calf's mouth, squeezed the plastic bottle and massaged her throat to encourage swallowing. In seconds the starving baby was nursing in earnest. When the bottle was empty, Bill laid her on the ground.

Within two days, she was dashing to the gate when she heard me coming. At the time, perhaps it was only the bottle she loved, and the green flake of hay, but in those happy eyes, I was now her mama.

With strange misgivings, I realized Friday was only two days away, and I'd fallen for the ugly crossbreed we didn't want or need. It didn't matter now what she looked like. She was a calf I cared about. More important, she trusted me with the innocence of a child who knows a mother means comfort and love. I couldn't let Bill take her to the auction.

"But she's useless to us," he said, proud of the quality and uniformity of his beautiful Herefords. "What good is an out-cross?"

"You're the one who said she looks part Holstein," I reminded him, "like Valentine, our nurse cow, who isn't going to last forever. Maybe someday Tiger Lily can replace her."

"Tiger Lily?"

"Yes, well . . . yes. Becky and Jaymee dreamed up that name after looking at one of our *National Geographic* magazines. It had a whole section with photographs of lilies. They thought the Tiger Lily was the prettiest and decided that would be the perfect name for—"

"Tiger Lily?" he said again, taking such a deep drag on his pipe I expected the smoke to come out of his boots. "Whoever heard of a cow named Tiger Lily?"

"Nobody, till now." I smiled at him.

"Well, she's your responsibility," he said, and I could almost hear the unspoken words — Remember, I don't have time to be fixing baby bottles.

I knew Tiger Lily would be gentle, a placid creature that would be easy to handle, a quiet playmate perhaps for a three-and a five-year-old, and an animal that one day would grow into a beautiful cow. I was mistaken. Tiger Lily was trouble almost from the start. She jumped into water troughs, broke the valves and flooded the barns and corrals in the night. She got stuck under her fence and had to be dug out. She chased chickens and, one day, being overly inquisitive, she was even bitten on the nose by a rattlesnake. Her face ballooned and I spent the night holding ice packs in place and hoping the antidote we always kept on hand would save her. I had forgotten about the years that a mother must survive before a youngster is grown. But I grew to love her.

When tiny horns appeared on Tiger Lily's head, an itchy spot at their base drove her nearly crazy. Scratching the itch on the corral fence brought little relief. The gate latch was far more effective, and she found that, with a small twist of her head and horns, that the gate opened, welcoming her to the whole, wide world beyond. There, searching for her "mama" became Tiger Lily's goal.

One hot morning, I was stunned when the handle on our kitchen screen door rattled and Tiger Lily, now over 300 pounds, pushed her way in. Snorting, she poked her nose in the bread box, and scanned the breakfast table with her enormous brown eyes. Then she tried scratching her horns against the table, lifting it right off the floor.

Before Bill came in for lunch he discovered the porch furniture and the garbage pails scattered like leaves in the yard. He didn't say much. But finding the outside mirrors on his pickup smashed and lying on the ground when he returned to work was too much. "She'll have to go out to pasture with the yearling heifers," he ordered, "and live like a normal cow — behind barbed wire."

So at nine months, Tiger Lily joined our other cattle, even though Bill considered her the weed among the flowers of his herd.

Certainly she stood out, with her huge, gangly brown body, and long bony back and hips I could hang my jacket on. I went out to see her often and always found her grazing peacefully. She never forgot me. All I had to do was call, "Tiger Lily! Hi, girl. Remember me? I'm your mama," and she would moo and amble over to have the itchy place at the base of her horns scratched.

Even out in pasture, though, it wasn't unusual to find her in the mornings with her horns stuck in an aluminum gate or tangled in rusty barbed wire. "What a *klutz!*" Bill would groan, as he struggled to get her loose.

When she was three years old, Tiger Lily got into the biggest and most serious trouble of all. We faced a difficult calving season. Some of the babies were too big. Seven calves had died at birth, a danger when breeding young heifers to an unproven bull. But with careful monitoring through a night patrol, Bill, Scott and I had already saved twenty-one calves by getting to the heifer in time, roping her and, with a winch or chains and the Jeep, pulling the oversized baby out before it suffocated in the birth canal.

It was February, well below freezing, and my turn to take the patrol. At 1:05 a.m. I was heading for the calving pasture on my all-terrain motorcycle. Two of our best cows were ready to calve. So was Tiger Lily, who had matured into an enormous heifer with horns like eagle wings and an udder that could put the finest Holstein to shame.

The calving pasture was a mile and a half from the house. With a single headlight joggling wildly to blaze my way and a wool scarf protecting my face, I sped alongside barbed wire fences, bounced over rutted trails and unseen rocks, and jumped on and off the cycle to open and close endless gates. At last, straight ahead, eyes glowing like distant headlights etched against the night, lay the peaceful herd of pregnant bald-faced Herefords.

As they watched my approach, warm mists of breath rose from their nostrils like crystal balloons in the icy air. I cruised slowly among them, close enough to read the black numbers glinting on their yellow plastic ear-tags, yet far enough away so I wouldn't disturb them. As I anticipated, the "heavies" — Tags 317, 402 and Tiger Lily

— were not among them. All three had vanished, in quest of privacy in a mesquite grove or a distant corner of the pasture where deep gullies carved by summer rains offered a place to hide from the others and bring their calves into the world.

First I found Tag 317 who was resting quietly and chewing her cud, a reassuring sign that it might be morning before real labor began. I kept searching for the other two, rewarded at last by the sight of a steaming, wide-eyed newborn glistening under the beam of my headlight, and the mother, Tag 402, lowing softly, sniffing the new arrival with mounting enthusiasm. I rode quietly by, not wanting to disturb this precious moment of bonding.

But where was Tiger Lily?

My hands and feet were numb when I finally found her, trapped upside down, hooves in the air, in an old cement irrigation ditch. She had rolled into the tapered, vise-like tomb while struggling to deliver her too-big calf. There was blood everywhere, and the tips of her horns had snapped off in her frantic effort to escape. The still form of her newborn lay a few feet farther along the ditch — dead.

The pitiful sight of that bloodied calf, so close to his trapped mother, was more than I wanted to deal with at that troubling moment. So, straining, I dragged the poor little thing farther down the ditch. Then I ran back and sank to my knees beside Tiger Lily.

"Oh, Tiger," my voice broke, "why did this have to happen to you?"

Terror rimmed her soft brown eyes, and when I reached down over the edge and placed my hand on her velvet nose, a strangled moan rose from deep within her half-ton body. She was scarcely breathing. Real fear gripped me when I shined my flashlight on her gums. No longer pink, they now gleamed a ghostly gray. Pressure from the sloping sides of the ditch was crushing her lungs. God help her, I prayed. Tiger Lily was slowly smothering to death.

I streaked home on my cycle, icy tears freezing to my cheeks. However, I no longer noticed the cold or the sounds of the ricocheting rocks ripped from the earth by my hobnailed tires. All I could think of was Tiger Lily. By the time I reached the house, I knew what we had to do.

I rushed inside and woke Bill. "Honey, wake up! We're going to need the big tractor with the front-end loader. Hurry!" Then I woke Scott. "Get dressed!" I blurted. "It's Tiger Lily! She's dying!"

I ran to the barn for our eight-foot crowbar, burlap sacks, chains, ropes and an oxygen tank and threw everything into the back of our old Chevy Blazer. Then I jumped in, turned on the engine, and shoved my hands deep into my pockets, wishing the heater still worked — and I waited. What's taking them so long? I wondered. Then I saw Bill trying to thaw the ignition switch on the huge Ford tractor with his pipe lighter — and I knew.

It seemed forever until that engine roared to life. Scott came and jumped in beside me. "Let's go, Mom," he said. "It'll take Dad ten minutes to get there with that thing. We'll leave the gates open for him."

When we finally reached Tiger Lily, her eyes were closed. "I think she's dead," I murmured.

Scott grabbed the oxygen, clamped the huge rubber mask over her nose and mouth, and adjusted the pressure gauges to force air into her lungs. We heard nothing except the hissing of the tank and the distant drone of the slow-moving tractor.

"Here, hold the mask tight!" Scott ordered and jumped up for the crowbar. The screech of iron against cement shattered the night as he shoved the bar down the concrete slope and under Tiger Lily's body. Then, leaning his 220 pounds over the top, he pressed down. Tiger Lily gasped. One breath. Would it be enough?

When Bill pulled up with the tractor, Scott moved fast. He clamped chains around her legs, and tied ropes to the broken horns to support her head and neck. Bill pulled as close as he dared, and Scott hooked the lifesaving lines to the loader's bucket. "Take her away, Dad!" he yelled.

Hydraulics wheezed. The boom moved upward, lifting Tiger Lily out of the ditch and laying her gently on the ground. Her mouth opened. Her sides heaved. "She's breathing!" I called, almost in tears.

Bill waved. Scott unhooked the chains and said, "Come on, Tiger, get up!" He put a halter on her head and pulled, but we all knew Tiger Lily couldn't move.

Again the bucket descended. Steel teeth chewed into the frozen earth beneath her, and as Bill scooped up the cow for the dark journey home, Scott jumped into the bucket beside her.

The vet arrived at dawn. "Her calf was so large it broke her pelvis and caused nerve damage," he said after examining her. "I'm afraid she's paralyzed." Tiger Lily lay on the ground where Bill had placed her.

"Will she walk again, Doc?" he asked.

"There's always hope — if she lives." Doc's face clouded. "She'll need a lot of care, though, and have to be rolled over several times a day."

I knew Bill and Scott could do that. Thirteen hundred

pounds of cow was heavy, but they were used to heaving a couple of tons of hay on and off the feed wagon twice a day. At the same time — although Bill would never say so — he'd also grown accustomed to the big, homely cow, the one that looked so different out there in the fields.

Three days later, however, we were worried. Tiger Lily still wouldn't eat or drink. We took turns massaging her cold back legs, but there was no sign of movement — not even a quiver. Her eyes were shut. I could tell she wanted to die. After all, what did she have to live for? She was paralyzed, but worse than that, her calf was gone — and she knew from that terrible night that I was the one who had taken it from her. I stroked that place at the base of her horns and she pulled her head away. She no longer wanted any part of me.

Three days later, Scott came speeding up the road from the calving pasture on the three-wheeler. Stretched across his lap lay a newborn calf. It had absolutely no hair. Its skin was crimson.

"It's a twin," he said. "The mother was trying to kill it!"

The calf was tiny, perhaps thirty pounds. Average among our newborns was seventy-five pounds. As Scott stood the poor little thing on the ground, it trembled and bawled long and piteously.

Then a small miracle unfolded. Mooing softly, Tiger Lily answered. A calf was crying, calling for its mama. Is it mine? Tiger Lily might have wondered. Something was whispering deep inside her. She mooed again, and the hairless calf tottered toward her. When moist pink noses touched, Tiger Lily opened her eyes, raised her chin and began licking the tiny face. Soon the calf was nuzzling her ears, her neck, her warm shoulder, searching her sunken belly and rigid legs, until finally he found the warm milk.

By nightfall, Tiger Lily had drunk her water and eaten some hay for the first time. When I checked her before going to bed that night, she was contentedly chewing her cud. This calf needed her. He was someone for her to sniff, to lick and protect, even though she couldn't move. He was hers to rest her chin on while she slept. And who knows? Perhaps she thought it was her own — come back at last for mothering.

We named the calf the Hairless Wonder, which the children soon shortened to Hairy, then Harry. As Harry grew stronger, we could see his goal was to make his mama get up. He charged into her, kicked her, crashed into her neck, butted her in the rump, and plowed into her belly. Tiger Lily never seemed to mind. She simply lay there, patiently waiting for the next onslaught, and munched on her hay. Harry was forgiven every time.

When the calf tired, he sought shade near the barns, tractors and cattle chutes, too far from his anxious mother. Tiger Lily mooed, frothed and swung her head nervously from side to side. Somehow we had to provide shade for the calf right next to her. It was Scott who remembered the orange and green beach umbrella we put up by the pool every summer.

"That's perfect," I said, as I watched him hammer it into the ground beside Tiger Lily. Little Harry seemed to welcome the shade so close to his mama.

Everyone, except me, took turns rubbing aloe vera cream on Harry's sensitive skin and moving the umbrella to keep him in the shade. I wanted to help, but even though Tiger Lily couldn't move, she scared me now if I got too close to her calf. She would shake her jagged horns at me, or rock back and forth on her chest, snorting fiercely. Did she somehow blame me for what happened to her in the irrigation ditch? Or could it be she was afraid I would take this calf away from her, too, the way I'd taken her first calf away?

"You never know about animals," Bill said. "You should understand that."

No, I didn't understand. And deep down, somewhere in all that pain and hurt she felt, I knew she was still my cow — and that she loved me.

Three weeks passed and it was time to put Tiger Lily on her feet. Bill and Scott made a huge canvas sling, rolled her onto it, and hooked the sling to the bucket of the tractor. Once again, the front-end loader lifted the paralyzed cow, but this time only enough so the men could plant her hooves on the ground. Her wasted body shuddered, but she was upright at last, and Harry raced around, wild with anticipation. His mama was going to be okay.

Meanwhile, what a curious sight they made! Eastern relatives visited us that spring — most of them with astounding misconceptions of Arizona ranch life. Expecting Indians, coyotes, wolves and buffalo, they were stunned to be greeted instead by a huge brown cow suspended in a hammock from the boom of a five-ton blue Ford tractor. And if that wasn't enough, there was also the hairless calf at her side, sleeping in the shade of an orange and green beach umbrella.

For six weeks Tiger Lily hung by day and was lowered at night to rest. May arrived, the sling was removed, and the healed cow now stood unaided. But she wouldn't walk. As I stood back, because my presence was so troubling to her, Bill and Scott pushed, pulled and shoved. They placed her food and water just out of reach, but the next morning she was still riveted to the same spot.

"I have an idea," Bill said to me one day. "Since she really seems to have it in for you, we'll chase Harry, and you make a grab for him. Maybe she'll take a step trying to protect him." Would she think I would take Harry away, the way she seemed to think I'd taken her first baby?

Bill and Scott gave chase. Sure enough. Tiger Lily began snorting and pawing with a front hoof. Disregarding how upset she really was, I grabbed Harry as he went spinning by. He squealed — loudly. The next thing I knew Tiger Lily's head struck me from behind and I was on the ground, my mouth full of sand. I felt like I'd been hit by a truck — and I was crushed.

"Hey, Mom!" Scott yelled. "It worked! She walked!" He and Bill tried not to laugh as they helped me up. Then they praised Tiger Lily for "being such a good girl." Grudgingly, I had to agree.

For the next seven months, Tiger Lily, with Harry at her side, lived an idyllic life as her calf grew a fine fur coat and soon reached 600 pounds. "Tiger Lily's going to make a fine nurse cow," said Bill. "Now the next step is to get her bred."

Then the day came for Harry to be weaned, and the loss of the calf that had given her a second chance at life devastated Tiger Lily. She lost 100 pounds. This poor, downtrodden weed among all the flowers of our herd spent days calling for Harry. I wanted to comfort her, but I still couldn't get near. Once again her calf had been taken from her — and she wanted nothing to do with me.

A year went by and Tiger Lily gave birth to twin heifers. They thrived on her rich, abundant milk, as did a third calf who came to "rob" her every few hours because his own mother didn't have enough.

At long last Tiger Lily seemed content. She was

needed, and a pattern was set for the next fifteen years. During this time, she raised sixteen calves of her own and countless foster offspring including the never-ending parade of hungry robbers who wanted just a little bit more.

Tiger Lily was almost twenty years old when arthritis in her back legs finally became so severe we knew we would soon have to put her down. One day, it seemed she sensed the last summer had come when she saw me putting up a brand new orange and green beach umbrella by the pool. The old cow began the long painful walk across the field in my direction. Suddenly, something stirred within me, the memory of a frightened, motherless orphan that walked into my life so long ago. I fought back tears as she moved closer, her back bowed like a much used hammock, her bony hips — airplane wings — and her brow a crown of crooked horns.

Then she was there, her head stretching over the fence, mooing softly to me. It was the moment I'd been waiting for. She had been my cow, and deep in my heart I always hoped that, despite the pain and hurt, she still loved me.

"Hi, old girl. Remember me?"

She looked up then with those soft brown eyes and very slowly lowered her head. I recognized the signal from all those years before. She wanted me to scratch the spot that itched at the base of her horns. I knew then I was forgiven . . . and today we all remember Tiger Lily — the stray that wandered into our hearts, a weed among her kind — who became the favorite flower in our fields.

February 10, 1985

I often think if anyone reads these diary entries fifty years from now, they won't understand what I'm talking about because there are so many words indigenous to where we live. One is "wash." It took an editor to teach me to use the word "arroyo" instead when writing. An arroyo is a "wash," a dry river bed that might have water in it only once in ten years — never — or every year. The water might run for an hour or several days. Some can even bring tremendous floods during the monsoon season.

At Singing Valley, we are bounded by washes. One has been called a The White River "draw" for years. Because so much overflow irrigation water from valley farms flows into it, it has become a permanent lake where whooping cranes visit seasonally, and cinnamon teal and mallard ducks nest and pass the summer. The White River draw is where we first saw our great blue heron ten years ago.

"Blue" stood nearly four feet tall. He was silver, and he wore the black crest on the top of his white head backwards, like a baseball cap. We passed this proud bird every morning on our way to the school bus. Except for occasional vultures, he was the only bird that seemed to stay all year around. We began to wonder why he didn't go home with his flock. Then our veterinarian told us what he believed was Blue's story.

Like all large birds, the heron mates for life. Perhaps his mate had been shot or injured. Perhaps a starving coyote dared to leap into the water one night while the pair was sleeping. We'll never know, but Blue stood alone in the White River draw for ten long years — watching the sky — waiting for his love to return.

Bill posted **NO HUNTING** *and* **NO TRESPASSING** *signs all over the ranch, but yesterday he caught two hunters laden with "ducks" hurrying to their truck. "No, I didn't see Blue in their catch," he said. But our lone heron was gone today. The girls and I hope he finally flew away . . . but a small voice within me says otherwise. The only consolation I find is . . . he doesn't have to wait any longer.*

A COYOTE NAMED PROMISE

I awoke to a violent, unearthly cry — like the sobs of a tortured demon.

At Singing Valley Ranch, night sounds are common: the screech of a great horned owl, the yowl of a bobcat, the electrifying squeal of bats racing the dawn. But for sheer shock value, nothing could equal this terrifying din of voices right beneath my window. It made me sit bolt upright in bed, my heart pounding. The clamor was soul-piercing — and unmistakable. Coyotes!

The coyote's eleven-note voice ranges from a high-pitched, hysterical shriek to a low, haunting howl. A single animal can sound like a pack of eight, two like sixteen, and when the voices of four echo against the distant mountains and cliffs it's like a symphony gone wild.

At Singing Valley Ranch, we rarely saw a coyote. It might have been because a Mexican lobo had staked out our land a long time ago and kept the coyotes at bay. Or maybe we ourselves had simply frightened coyotes off with our noisy all-terrain motorcycles.

Whatever the reason, I found myself missing the magic of this shy, illusive creature gliding through the tall gamma grasses or slinking among our manzanita bushes. Although hunger prompted his predatory ways, the coyote had become a dim memory for my husband Bill and me — except on moonlit nights when an eerie howl resonated from far off arroyos and mountain tops, reminding us he was still out there somewhere.

Now, as the fiendish howls reached an ear-splitting crescendo, I sat a long moment in bed. Then, as quickly as all the commotion started, it stopped. I reached over and pulled back the edge of the striped serape covering the window, expecting to see a battleground strewn with dead cats, dogs, chickens — perhaps a newborn calf. Instead, a telltale quivering of pyracantha bushes, a scattering of orange-red berries and tufts of rabbit fur strewn like dandelion down provided the only vague clues to one of nature's desperate struggles for survival.

There'd been a coyote out there — I knew this for sure. My gaze shifted to Bill on his tractor over a mile away. His headlights were still on as the early-morning mist crawled over the lush green fields. He'd been cutting alfalfa since 4 a.m., and the day before he'd oiled, tightened and sharpened the sixty-three sets of gleaming, scissor-like blades on the swather, a sixteen-foot-long mower he attached to the side of the tractor with the help of our grown son, Scott. I wondered, did he see the animal? The tractor vanished into the ghostly fog.

The coyote was far from my thoughts as I prepared breakfast for Becky and Jaymee, now twelve and nine. They had been outside feeding their 4-H calves and rabbits before school. Suddenly, Jaymee burst into the kitchen, horror in her eyes. "Mama!" she yelled. "Daddy killed a coyote! Just now, out in the field, I saw it thrown in the air!"

My thoughts flew back to those frenzied howls of less than two hours before. They still sent a chill through me. Could that have been the animal Bill had killed? "Are you sure?" I asked Jaymee, trying to ease her fears. "You know for sure it was a coyote? You were so little when they used to be around here."

"But I know what coyotes look like!" Jaymee persisted. "I saw one on the highway, and when Becky and I were riding with Scott near the mountains, we saw two of them. They were gray and brown and black with huge, bushy tails and just a little smaller than a German shepherd." A deep frown angled between her eyebrows. "I know what one looks like, Mama. And this was a coyote."

Much later, when Bill came in for breakfast he hung his sweat-stained hat on the rack and sank into his chair by the wood stove. "I think I clobbered a coyote," he said.

"I know. Jaymee told me." I could see how much this bothered him.

"For the past few days, I've seen a coyote watching me from the edge of the field — a pitiful-looking creature, scrawny and sick. I saw her once in the rearview mirror catching mice behind the baler. She didn't seem the least bit afraid. Now this had to happen." He was silent for a moment. "I looked all over for her, but she must have dragged herself off and died in some other part of the field."

"How do you know it was a she?"

"Big old belly," he said, sighing. "Pregnant."

I shuddered. "Maybe you just thought you killed her."

He shot me a hard glance. "Look, it's over and she's dead," he said. "All we can do now is watch for the buzzards to circle around and pinpoint where her body is. Then I'll get rid of it before cutting and baling the rest of the field."

The buzzards, however, never appeared. Could the coyote still be alive? I wondered. Maybe it's still out there somewhere, suffering. I couldn't stop thinking about it.

Summer slipped into autumn and thoughts of the coyote dimmed. Winter closed in. Now hunger stalked the wild animals on the surrounding desert. In search of food, they moved closer to our barns, corrals and outbuildings. Often at night, while checking on pregnant heifers for signs of labor, I caught sight of a hooded skunk, or a coatimundi (a monkey-like animal of the raccoon family) or a porcupine emerging for a starlit shuffle searching for a forgotten kernel of corn or a tree where a few remaining leaves or a cocoon could be found.

January arrived with a vengeance, bringing icy winds, heat lamps in the henhouse, a need for blankets on the horses, the calving season — and the return of the coyote. It was midnight when I heard the first diabolical shrieks and howls near my chicken coop. I dressed quickly and dashed outside. There in the beam of my light, I met her face to face: an old coyote — with three legs. The left hind leg was missing below the knee.

So Bill's tractor took only her leg, I thought. But how did she survive? Could she still catch a rabbit? She was less than a shadow, a pathetic, skeletal creature with coarse, gray ratty-looking fur. The once-bushy tail was mangy and shredded, and she looked at me with such a woebegone expression it tore at my heart.

And what about her baby? If it had lived, the pup would be weaned by now and was probably eight or nine months old. I glanced around but didn't see it.

Enormous ears cupped the coyote's dainty, intelligent face. Although she showed neither fear nor surprise, I sensed something was terribly wrong. Then she tilted her head into the shaft of light and I saw her aged amber eyes. Veiled in cataracts, they glowed like tiny blue gas jets in the darkness. Poor, poor thing, I thought. That's why she got hurt. She's probably blind.

I wanted to reach out, step a little closer, but this was a wild thing. Can she see at all? I wondered.

As if in answer to my thoughts, her lips parted, revealing a flash of smile — and fangs. I knew now she could see something, but I also sensed she was not alone because she was reacting like any mother animal would, protecting her young against strangers. Perhaps her pup was nearby.

We stared at each other, neither of us moving, until gradually I felt a rare bond of trust pass between us before she finally turned and hobbled off into the night. At that moment, I grasped the full extent of the tragedy that had befallen her. Maybe Bill was right. Perhaps we should have hunted her down and put her out of her misery. Overwhelmed with pity, I flicked off the light so she could shrink unobserved into the moonlit shadows.

What can I do? I asked myself. I didn't care that she was a predator and a threat to small livestock. She was starving to death. Her natural diet was birds, rodents, rabbits and insects. But I had also heard that coyotes like fruit. Maybe she'll eat dog food with apple slices on top, I thought.

I couldn't help wondering what Duke would think of that. Duke was our timid, 206-pound English mastiff, and he ate and slept on the front porch only a few feet from where this same coyote had killed a rabbit all those months before. He let the barn cats finish his food; but how would he feel about this wild animal eating from his bowl? I had to try. So I prepared the first bowlful.

A short time later, back in bed, I heard strange sounds outside the front door. Peeking beneath the striped serape, I saw the wild and the tame, hair raised, tails clamped, cowering on opposite sides of the bowl. Although a single lunge from Duke could crush the crippled coyote, the confrontation unleashed a torrent of voices instead. The coyote, ears pinned back and crouched low on her belly, was yapping and scolding while Duke, afraid to take his eyes off her, trembled and whined. Finally, he sank heavily to the ground, dropped his huge head between his paws and moaned while the coyote crept toward his bowl and dug in.

When I told Bill the good news, he shook his head.

"It's not right," he said. "This is a wild animal that's now weak and can't take care of herself. We should put her out of her misery — or at least let nature take its course. We shouldn't be interfering."

"She has survived this long," I countered. "If it's survival of the fittest, maybe she is the fittest! We're just giving her a little help."

Several times during the following three months, the coyote appeared. And as she fed at Duke's bowl, I was always aware of a mournful howl from the barren plains to the north. Could it be her pup crying for her? Or possibly the father of her pup? Coyotes mate for life and the yearning wail was almost heart-moving in its plea.

Eight weeks after her first feeding at Duke's bowl, I noticed a glint of brownish red and black tinting her silver-gray fur. And her body was filling out a little more. One morning I told the girls, "Our coyote looks much healthier. I think she's going to make it!"

"You promise?" Becky asked.

"Promise," I said, crossing my fingers. But the same question still nagged. As Bill had said, was it really fair to interfere with the laws of nature and prolong a life of agony? I was still searching for an answer when Jaymee, who liked to give every living creature on the ranch a name, smiled at me. "Oh, Mama," she said. "That's perfect. Let's call her 'Promise.'"

An unusually wet spring brought swarms of flying beetles, moths and flies that clung to the screen door like barnacles. When they started slipping into the house every time the door opened, Bill installed a zapper light. When the bugs hit the electrically charged mesh, they sparked and fizzed, then spiraled down onto the concrete in smoldering piles. Barn cats arrived in droves to feast on them.

Then one evening before I'd put extra food out for Promise, the familiar shrieking and yodeling began. We all peered through the living-room window and saw Promise snapping eagerly at the smoking bugs in mid-air and gobbling them down.

"I'll bet she likes them cooked, better than raw," Jaymee murmured, and I saw Bill peer over the top of his newspaper. The laughter in his eyes said he was becoming more and more intrigued by this animal he didn't think should survive, but had survived. A few days later, he bought a book that told us how, in times of drought and famine, the cunning coyote will outlast all creatures because he is a digger of wells. When smaller animals and birds come to his well to drink, the coyote pounces.

Promise appeared only one more night after that, and

I saw she was pregnant again. Her fur was thick and shiny now, her tail magnificently bushy.

From Bill's book, we learned that Promise — being pregnant — was the number-one female of her pack, the only one producing offspring. Experts believe the lead female emits a hormonal odor that induces other females not to ovulate.

Late in her pregnancy, the coyote holes up in a den burrowed by a smaller animal and now revamped to suit her size and needs. There she is fed by her mate and other members of the pack — but only until her pups are weaned. After that, Promise would be on her own again.

Soon I noticed a change in Bill. It began one day when he left a patch of alfalfa uncut. "Another dumb duck built her nest out there," he mumbled. Then a week later a jackrabbit sat in the alfalfa and defied him. So once more, Bill's straight-arrow cutting veered off at an angle.

Finally, one scorching day in August, Bill had an even bigger surprise when he was baling. A three-legged coyote appeared on the edge of the field — with a young pup. Promise hobbled toward the tractor, totally unafraid.

As Bill watched, a memorable thing happened. When the baler scooped up the windrows, field mice suddenly lost their hiding places beneath the rows of neatly stacked hay, and the pup began chasing them. After the pup had eaten several mice, Promise waited until he caught another — then she grabbed her offspring by the neck and threw him to the ground. He let go of the mouse in his mouth and she ate it herself. As mother and son took off single file and lay down near the edge of the field, Bill marveled at what he'd seen.

"Did they go to sleep?" Becky asked at dinner that evening when Bill told us the story.

"Not right away," he said, "at least, not the pup." Now his voice took on a new, warmer tone when he talked about the mother and baby coyote. "He had to chew on her nose for a while, nipped at her ears and face. But he finally curled up right next to her and settled down. She looked so darned content, just like your Mama did when you kids were little and finally fell asleep." Bill glanced at me and grinned.

As winter approached, we wondered what would happen when our crippled coyote weaned her pup and the pack no longer took special care of her. Would she turn to us again?

Each night, I put extra food in Duke's bowl with slices

of apple on top. It was still there in the morning. But distant howling and shrieking were more prevalent than in the past. Was it Promise? Her two pups? Her pack?

The months hurried by and alfalfa season came again. More and more, Bill's quarter-mile windrows zigged and zagged. When I commented on the scattered patches of uncut green dotted with lavender blossoms, he grumbled, "I had to steer around a quail's nest and a couple of darn rabbits." But the sudden twinkle in his eyes said a few detours were okay.

It was near the end of April when he saw a coyote bounding along beside him, inches from the razor-sharp blades. It was a female — young, healthy and pregnant. "She followed me for over an hour," Bill told us. "She wasn't the least bit scared of me or the tractor. And she caught mice like an old pro."

An old pro? Could this have been another of Promise's pups, one I had never seen? Had she witnessed, from her hiding place in the shadows near a chicken coop, my first meeting with Promise? Had she watched the next summer as her mother and younger brother caught mice in our fields?

That night I heard a coyote howl and recalled Promise's amber eyes veiled in blue, a small sad face and quick flash of teeth. I realized then what a stalwart our crippled coyote really was. Against tremendous physical odds, the threat of nature and of man, Promise had raised her pups.

"I guess you were right," Bill said, grinning at me. "They are survivors, aren't they?"

"Yes," I said, smiling. Promise had taught us both something about hardship, perseverance and the value of a helping hand. No wonder coyotes have so much to sing about.

And if we can remember those same lessons, we have a lot to sing about too.

May 20, 1978

Today Jaymee is eight. On birthdays we eat dinner at Mike's Corral, a steakhouse down Frontier Road. There are very few restaurants in Cochise County, but eating out is a real treat and, for the girls, indeed an unparalleled adventure. Since it's always a long drive wherever we go, the first thing Becky and Jaymee have to do is dash to the restroom. They are usually gone for quite a long time. When they return, the conversation centers on the ladies' room: what color the walls are, the curled-up floor tiles, no toilet paper except on the floor, messy sinks, no paper towels, and the "nasty, sloppy ladies" who throw everything on the floor. But mostly they remember the writing on the walls and tidings etched on the doors.

Becky must have a photographic mind because on their return, she remembers and recites every word she saw. Tonight, when we stopped to eat at an unfamiliar diner on our way back from hauling a horse to Lordsburg, New Mexico, Bill wasn't in the mood for "ladies room" talk.

"That's enough, Beck," he growled as she and Jaymee cuddled extra close on the opposite side of the booth. "Pick out what you want to eat."

They scanned the menu. "I'll have a hamburger and fries, please," Becky said. Then, heads touching, she and Jaymee returned to the news on the bathroom walls: "Maria loves Fernando," " Jesus is Lord," " Jorgé loves Francesca," but it was "Rachel sat here" that sent them off into such hysteria that tears poured down their faces. I'm almost glad Bill is a little hard of hearing for I swear these children have a conspiracy of sorts between them. But he told me later he found it hard not to laugh too.

WITH A LITTLE LUCK

"Daddy! Look what I found!" Jaymee ran to Bill, her small hands cupping a hidden treasure.

"What is it, honey?" Bill looked down at our youngest daughter and mopped his forehead. The late summer heat was oppressive. Mother Nature wasn't being kind to southeastern Arizona. Drought had withered our pastures. Bill was running the pumps twenty-four hours a day to irrigate the crops. He still had calves to vaccinate and hay to bale. This wasn't his day. Lately no day was.

Cautiously, Jaymee unfolded her hands. Cradled there was a tiny hours-old jackrabbit.

"Can I keep him, Daddy?"

Jaymee, then eight, had wanted a pet rabbit for years, but Bill, of course, was a rancher and already had a filly picked out for her. He hadn't bargained on her liking rabbits more than heifers and horses.

"It'll die," he said. "Babies need a mama."

"Can't I try? Please?" Jaymee begged. "You always say, 'With a little luck, anything's possible.'"

Bill sighed. He couldn't stand more problems now. The doctor had told him to slow down and learn to relax a little.

Jaymee turned to me, tears threatening. "Let's take him in the house," I said softly.

Cally, one of several calico cats, was nestled near the wood stove with her seven new kittens. Was it possible to trick Mother Nature? I wondered.

Jaymee and I fed Cally until she was stuffed. When her eyes closed and purring began, Jaymee pushed the jackrabbit's searching mouth against an untapped nipple. The tiny creature clung like peanut butter to a spoon. For three days, he grew fatter, and Cally seemed to treat him like one of her own.

"See, Daddy. It's true — with a little luck, anything's possible."

But on the fourth day, Cally looked at this "kitten" through slit eyes, and then a wail of anger filled the kitchen. Her jaws opened and she pounced. Bill leaped up, grabbed Cally by the tail, and the interloper tumbled from her claws.

Bill scooped up the trembling creature and gave it to Jaymee. "Better try bottle-feeding him," he said.

Miraculously, the jack rabbit lived. Soon he was eating

cereal — and growing and growing. Finally, we set him free, happy knowing he had another chance at life.

Jaymee, petless again, resumed her campaign. "Please, Daddy, can't I have just one little rabbit, a tame one this time?"

Bill looked at me for help. "What good is a rabbit?" he asked.

Jaymee's eyes grew round. "They bring luck!"

I knew it would take more than that to sway Bill Porter.

"Oh, please, Daddy? I'd join 4-H and show it like you do with the cattle and horses." She came closer, her brown eyes tugging at his heart. Suddenly her arms were around his neck, and in one quick movement she slipped a bag of jelly beans into his pocket. Jaymee knew jelly beans helped more than anything. And they helped now.

That weekend, we drove to Albuquerque where Bill bought three New Zealand Reds, all females.

"Why three?" I asked quietly.

"A little extra luck," he whispered, glancing in the rearview mirror at the happy girl in the back seat.

"Their names are Twinkletoes, Marshmallow and

Alice," Jaymee called, holding the bunnies up one at a time for her father to see. "And Daddy, they'll bring you lots of good luck. I promise!"

Three months later, Twinkletoes gave birth to six babies. Then Marshmallow produced eight. We were stunned.

"How did they get pregnant, Mama?" Jaymee asked. "They haven't been near a buck. And why didn't Alice get pregnant too?"

"The rabbit dealer made a mistake," I offered.

"He lied is what he did," Bill said. "Seventeen rabbits!"

"That means lots of luck!" Jaymee announced, trying to soften the blow.

Bill renamed "Alice" Abraham, which in Hebrew means "Father of the many," and secured him behind dividers on the east wall of the hutch.

Then our twelve-year-old nephew, George, visited from Milwaukee. George hated cows and horses. But he loved Abraham. Two weeks after he went home, Twinkletoes produced a litter of nine, and Marshmallow, eleven. Once more, Bill was exasperated. "All right," he said, "how'd it happen this time?"

"It was George," said Jaymee. "He loved watching

them 'do it.'" She showed Bill her journal, with its neatly recorded transactions. Under "Item," the name George appeared. Under "Charge," twenty-five cents. Every day George had begged Jaymee to put Abraham in with Twinkletoes or Marshmallow. So she charged him twenty-five cents a half hour! At the bottom of a long column was "Grand Total, $4.75."

Jaymee now had thirty-seven rabbits. Bill put more dividers in the hutch. "We'll soon be ordering rabbit feed by the truckload!" he grumbled.

I pointed out that, with the rabbits' arrival, his luck was changing for the better. Cattle prices were up. We'd had the best alfalfa season ever, and the rain came.

"That has nothing to do with rabbits," he said.

Twinkletoes became Jaymee's favorite. She came when called and hopped on a collar and leash.

Then Twinkletoes got pregnant again, and this time no one asked how. What difference did it make? Cattle prices were staying up. As even Bill recognized, all was well.

But when it was time to give birth, Twinkletoes got sick and was unable to line her nest. She lay on the floor of the hutch gasping, each breath, we thought, her last. Eight babies arrived shortly after nightfall: wet, cold and barely alive.

"They're going to die, Daddy. What can we do?"

To my astonishment, he said, "Don't worry, honey," and handed each of us two icy newborns and shoved the other four in his pockets. To me he said, "Run and light the stove."

We lined a pizza pan with foil and wet paper towels and laid the seemingly lifeless kits in a circle. Covering them with another wet towel, we popped them into the oven, set at the lowest possible heat, and watched through the glass window as, one by one, the tiny lumps started to jerk and wiggle.

Jaymee beamed. "Just our luck," Bill said with a grin. Then he hugged her close.

Back in the hutch, Twinkletoes had made a remarkable recovery. We helped her pull fur from her chest so we could wrap up her babies and line the box.

By the next morning, eight warm bunnies were cuddled at the bottom of her nest. Bill, I could tell, was as proud as Jaymee that all had lived.

Eventually the day came when a buyer offered to purchase Jaymee's rabbits. She agreed to sell them — except for Twinkletoes.

Was it mere coincidence that Bill's luck suddenly soured? Cattle prices fell. Constant rains damaged the alfalfa. An irrigation well caved in.

Yet this time, Bill seemed different, more patient and relaxed. I wanted to believe it had something to do with a little girl and her rabbits. Perhaps not. But there could be no question that they had distracted him lately from his worries — and maybe reminded him that, above all, family is more important than horses and heifers.

Anyway, he had stopped complaining that the newspaper was always a day late and began commenting on sunrises at breakfast. He found time to take Jaymee up to the high school so she could see her sister play freshman volleyball. He visited and telephoned our three grown children more often now. Things that had gone wrong began to right themselves again.

One afternoon, Bill returned from Tucson, where he'd gone to buy a fuel pump for the tractor. When Jaymee and I went to meet him, Twinkletoes hopped happily beside us.

As Bill climbed out of the truck, a worried Jaymee asked, "Daddy, do you think Twinkletoes is too old to have babies?" We had taken her to a champion buck twice, with no luck.

Pulling a box from the truck, Bill paused and smiled at Twinkletoes. "No, sweetheart," he said. "Mother Nature has just given her a chance to enjoy other things."

"Like taking a walk on a leash?"

"Well sure — but more than that." Putting the box down, Bill leaned over and stroked the rabbit. "It's more like the happiness of knowing she's loved." He paused. "And knowing there's a big world out there that, with a little luck, she'll have time to enjoy."

He turned and opened the box. Suddenly his face darkened. "Damn!" he said. "They gave me the wrong pump. Now I'll have to drive 100 miles back to Tucson tomorrow."

"Can we go?" Jaymee asked. "It'll be Saturday. Mama's taking Becky to a horse show, so we could have lunch. Just the two of us."

Bill's expression softened. "You know," he said, "there's a new Mexican restaurant in Tucson. After we pick up the pump, let's go there. Should be fun."

When Bill went to wash up, he was smiling. I noticed something else too: before all the chores and problems began to get him down, he had always gone about humming to himself. Now that a little girl and her rabbits had brought a bit of luck back into his life, Bill was humming again.

September 22, 1981

The County Fair is next week — the highlight of the year. While all the mothers help their children with assorted 4-H projects like cooking, canning, sewing, arts and crafts and so on, excitement skyrockets in the Open and 4-H livestock divisions. The most coveted prize is the Blue Ribbon. Bill and Scott and other ranchers spend hours fitting prize cattle for show, sale and auction.

After halter breaking and teaching select bulls and heifers to lead on ropes by tying them to truck bumpers and tugging them around gently, they bathe and clip them daily. Finally, toenails are trimmed and horns sanded and polished till they gleam like marble.

The night before judging, they scrub the animals one more time with expensive livestock shampoo. A touch of bluing is used in the final rinse water to make the faces shine. Blow-drying a 1000-pound animal with an oversized hair dryer takes hours. The bulls love it; they close their eyes in ecstasy. Bill and Scott clip and comb the hide against the grain so it stands out straight like sheared beaver. Finally, the tip of the foot-long white tail is teased into a perfect round ball, sprayed with a show shellac, then protected with a plastic bag over the ball to keep it perfect until ring time.

Most of the kids raise a steer (a castrated bull). They are all excited about selling it and making big money at the auction after the show. At the end of the long day, however, the kids are not only exhausted but they suddenly realize the "pet" they have loved and raised for nearly a year is headed for the freezer. It's sad to see these kids, faces buried in soft fur, sobbing their hearts out in the sale barn. Bill is determined Becky and Jaymee will raise a calf when they are old enough. I hope he gives them a heifer. Then we can keep it to replenish the herd, or sell it to another rancher for breeding.

BRINGING UP BUTTERCUP

"Where were you?"

Bill hung his weathered Stetson on the bullhorn rack by the wood stove, lit his pipe, and through a cloud of Cherry Blend, fixed his eyes on our twelve-year-old daughter.

Becky, deep in an algebra assignment at the kitchen table, didn't even look up. She only gripped her pencil tighter. "I couldn't come out and help, Daddy," she said. "I'll get extra credit if I do all these equations."

Bill ruffled her honey-blond hair. "Well, we sure could have used an extra hand on that corral gate. Then those cows wouldn't have broken through the darn fence."

His tone was gentle, but I knew he was concerned about Becky. She was too much like he used to be. Bill had been a math whiz himself, earning an engineering degree and planning a lucrative career. But his time as a POW during World War II changed his thinking. Back home, he chose to be an Arizona rancher. He could spend more time doing what he now considered more important

—drawing closer to his family and the land. In particular, he enjoyed cattle and wanted his children to share that experience.

Two of our older children, Bud and Scott, showed bulls and heifers at county fairs. Our youngest, Jaymee, could hardly wait until she was old enough to do the same. But Becky loved numbers. She'd rather count cows than raise one.

Bill, however, refused to give up. "Wouldn't you like to show your very own yearling heifer next year?" he asked Becky one day. "You could win a blue ribbon!"

"I'm too busy, Daddy. I've got tests coming up. And I help other kids in math."

"Come on, honey. I'll give you the calf out of my best cow. When it's ready to show, you can sell it and keep the money for college." Reluctantly Becky followed Bill into his office. He sifted through pedigree notebooks that listed dozens of names, each identified with eight-digit numbers. "Here she is! Tag 333. A beautiful heifer. Look at these bloodlines! Her baby will be one heck of a calf!"

When Becky checked the pedigree, a smile brightened her face. I was surprised. Then, just as suddenly, I understood. It was all those numbers beneath Tag 333's name and the same long combinations under the ancestors that cued her to say, "Okay, Daddy. I'll give it a try."

In the following weeks, she started a journal of projected expenses: vaccinations, registration fees, vet bills, grain and hay.

"She's finally getting interested in cattle," Bill told me happily.

I wasn't so sure. For Becky, the calf project seemed more like a mathematical challenge. The living, breathing animal that would require constant care, training, love — and stall cleaning — never seemed part of the picture.

Something else gnawed at me. Unlike most Herefords, Tag 333 was a crazy thing with wild, popping eyes, flaring nostrils and horns like grappling hooks. Her fluorescent yellow ear tag flashed her I.D. number — 333 — like a warning signal.

She soared over barbed-wire fences into neighbors' pastures. She bolted into chutes backward and flipped over. Then there were her adventures with the squeeze, the chute that immobilizes the cow for its own protection and the safety of the handlers; suddenly Tag 333 would lie down in the squeeze and have to be pried out with crowbars before she suffocated. Instead of being grateful, she'd leap over the steel-paneled corral fences, inspiring the rest of the herd to do the same.

"Best pedigree in the herd," Bill still claimed to

anyone he could corner.

"Aren't you worried that cow might reject her baby?" I asked Bill. "Don't you think she's a little bit . . . loco?"

"Her mama had six calves and no problems," he replied. "It's all in the genes."

On a darker than usual February night, as we climbed into bed, Bill said, "Tag 333's due to calve any time now."

I scrunched down under the covers. "Well, let's hope she doesn't have it tonight," I said. "Did you see the TV weather forecast? It's supposed to get really cold."

Soon his familiar snore left me alone with my misgivings — not only about the weather, but about Becky and how she'd do, raising Tag 333's calf. Isn't it strange, I started thinking. Bill couldn't see beyond those precious genes. They might promise long legs and the better beef density that cattlemen always looked for in the Hereford breed, but why did he seem to forget that Tag 333 was also a rancher's nightmare, bounding over fences and flipping upsidedown in chutes? Didn't genes affect personality too?

The next morning, as dawn filtered through our bedroom windows, I woke up still stewing. Then I heard Bill call, "Penny. Come see this! Hurry!"

I jumped out of bed, hugging myself for warmth, and joined him in the kitchen.

"The temperature went down to twenty below zero last night," he said, pointing out the window. "A seventy-five-degree drop in twenty-four hours."

Winter's magic had transformed our pastures into a fairyland. Icicles clung like strings of festive lights along miles of irrigation. Cattle huddled in scattered bunches, steam rising like woodsmoke from their broad backs. Bulls stood alone, heads low, dignity gone. Small calves shivered at their mothers' sides. Calves! My heart leapt. "What about Tag 333?" I asked Bill.

He frowned. "We can't find her. Scott's checking some of the other pastures."

I lit the stove and woke Becky and Jaymee for school. They were eating breakfast when we heard the crunch of heavy boots. Scott burst into the kitchen.

"Can't find that cow, Dad. But I saw her calf about a mile down field, frozen up against an irrigation wheel . . . and . . . ." He glanced quickly at Becky, then back at his father. "It doesn't look good. You better bring the truck. I'll go ahead on the three-wheeler."

Piling into the pickup beside Bill, we followed Scott, a red flash streaking across the frosted land astride his all-terrain motorcycle. By the time we reached the calf, he was already punching away the icicles imprisoning the calf's rigid body.

"It's a little heifer," he murmured.

Glazed in ice, the newborn was frozen fast to the ground, her head wedged between the spokes of a giant irrigation wheel. Her eyes, sealed beneath long white lashes, glittered with chunks of frost.

"Damn cow, " Bill muttered. "Takes off and leaves her baby to freeze to death. I should have gotten rid of her . . ."

Too late, I thought.

"Is she dead?" Becky asked.

Scott shook his head. "I don't know, Beck." He pulled off a glove and pressed his fingers against the calf's chest. "No heartbeat, Dad."

"Let's get her to the barn — fast!" Bill gripped the back legs, Scott the front, and they ripped the seventy-pound calf from the earth and swung her into the truck. She struck the metal bed like a slab of granite.

"Geez! She's frozen solid," said Scott, jumping in beside her. To get her circulation going, he began rubbing her body with a burlap sack. "Let's go. I'll get the bike later."

As the rest of us climbed into the pickup, Becky leaned forward to wipe a circle where breath had fogged the windshield. "Oh no!" she cried, pointing straight ahead at the brown and white chunks of fur and skin frozen to the spokes of the irrigation wheel. "We left pieces of her ears behind!"

In the straw-filled stall, the calf lay motionless. Bill thumped and squeezed the calf's legs and rib cage while Scott searched for a vein in her neck so he could start an I-V.

Becky watched quietly, red mittens pressed over her mouth. "What can I do, Daddy?" she asked.

"Go find some heavy horse blankets. We've got to get her warm." Bill lifted the calf's eyelid. "This youngster isn't dead yet."

Scott gave a whoop. "We've got a heartbeat, and the I-V's working!"

I hurried to the house for colostrum — first milk — that we kept for emergencies. A few drops in the calf's mouth, and the tiny jaws moved slightly. Soon the tug on the bottle told me she was nursing.

Becky sank to her knees in the golden straw beside me. She'd taken off her mittens. Now she reached out to stroke the calf's cold, white face and run her fingers over the torn and ragged ears. "You're going to be all right," she whispered. "I know you are."

But Bill, Scott and I knew the dangers, even if the calf survived: pneumonia, kidney damage, arthritis. So I was glad to hear Bill say, "Becky, she's not out of the woods yet. But if she doesn't make it, I'll help you pick another calf."

"I don't want another one, Daddy. Besides, I've already named her: Buttercup." The unexpected emotion in her voice startled us.

The furrows between Bill's eyebrows suddenly deepened. "That's a nice name, honey," he said. "I like it."

The calf was in a deep sleep. Scott hung the I-V from a rafter. "Can I stay with her?" Becky asked. "She might wiggle out from the covers."

When I went back to check later, Becky and Buttercup were both under the blankets.

After lunch, Scott removed the I-V. The calf was shivering violently by now. Becky gave her a bottle. At the four o'clock feeding, the calf's brown eyes were bright with anticipation. "Look," Becky said. "She knows me."

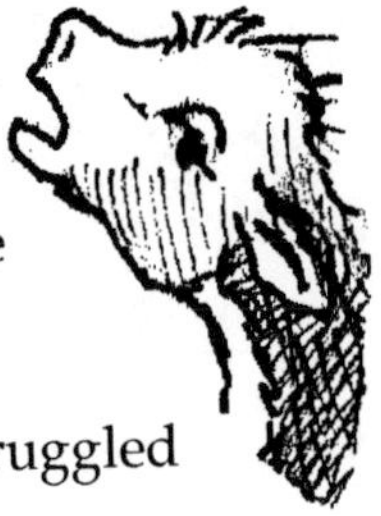

Eager to nurse, the little creature struggled

to stand, but her legs were still jackknifed beneath her. All she could do was flop around. Then she'd look up at Becky and bawl.

The next morning, I found the calf was buttoned into one of Bill's old sweaters. Becky, I quickly realized.

"How'd you get her legs through those sleeves?" I asked. "They won't unbend."

"She let me straighten them by myself and, after a while, they'll stay straight, Mama. I know they will." But straw and blankets had been tossed everywhere, evidence of the calf's all-night battle to stand. Please, I prayed, don't let Becky get too attached.

We were leaving for the school bus when Bill spoke softly to Scott. "We'll take care of that calf first thing." Becky knew what that meant, but as I drove to the bus stop she said, "Daddy will think of something."

When I got home, Bill and Scott were heading for the barn. I turned up the radio to drown out the crack of the rifle. After an hour I went to check. "Steady, girl," I heard Bill say. I looked into the stall. The calf's legs were wrapped in cotton batting and splints made from plastic pipe. Buttercup was standing.

By the end of the day, Buttercup was walking. After school, Becky put a halter on her and they toured the barnyard. Two weeks later, Scott removed the splints.

Although her knees still trembled and swelled, Buttercup continued to walk. But now her fight against respiratory illnesses began.

Over the next three months, Becky's columns of medical expenses lengthened. Bill looked at her journal and groaned. "At this rate," he said, "Buttercup's going to be the most valuable cow on the ranch. She better bring a bundle at the fair." But I knew he was pleased Becky seemed to care.

But does she really? I wondered. Now and then, I began thinking so, until summer arrived along with a chance to sleep late. But Becky had to care for Buttercup. "Why does she have to be fed at six o'clock, Mama?" she pleaded. "What's wrong with eight? It's vacation."

There was no question at all about Buttercup's feelings toward Becky. While Bill and Scott struggled to halter-break young bulls and heifers, Buttercup now happily followed Becky around the ranch.

Summer passed, and fall and winter slid into spring. At thirteen months, Buttercup weighed close to 500 pounds. She now had huge brown eyes, four white socks and a coat that shone like mahogany. Although tiny horns jutted above her ragged ears, she didn't show any of her mother's unwanted traits.

Becky was determined to win that blue ribbon in September. "A show calf has to be perfect," Bill warned. But he hung the yellow I.D. tag on the worst of Buttercup's ears to disguise the damage.

Becky began shampooing and brushing the ears every day. "Hair will cover the notches by September," she said. "She'll be almost perfect." I could see that wonderful little accountant's mind clicking like a calculator, adding up the days.

July brought deadly heat, a profusion of flies and pink eye, a blinding scourge of white-faced cattle. The disease prowled through the herds like a thief in the night, striking at random and stealing the sight of the healthiest cows. One morning, six weeks before the fair, Becky found Buttercup's face stained with tell-tale rivers of muddy tears. A closer look revealed the swollen lids and white, unseeing eyes of the disease. Even with antibiotic therapy, recovery could take up to two months. "Daddy," Becky pleaded, "can you make her well in time?"

"We'll have to try." Together, Bill and Becky prepared the medicine and glued black patches over the heifer's eyes to protect them from glare, flies and dirt.

A week before the show, the patches were removed.

We held our breath as Becky crouched in front of Buttercup. "All the brown's come back in her eyes," she said happily. "She can see!"

Flags, mariachis, shouting children and bawling cattle added to the excitement at the Cochise County Fair. Judging day for cattle was Saturday. Buttercup was groomed and ready. So was Becky. At 3 p.m. she and the other contestants were waiting in line to show their heifers. Horns were polished, hoofs shellacked. Tails were teased and sprayed.

"She looks great, honey," Bill said. "Now don't forget, buyers are in the crowd. If she wins, you'll get an offer and she'll be gone —" he snapped his fingers "just like that." Bill was surprised Becky didn't show more excitement. Wasn't this the big moment she'd been working for?

The gate opened and Buttercup's competition entered the ring: five magnificent big-boned, long-legged heifers. "They make Buttercup look so small," I whispered to Bill.

The judge, a rangy Texan, began checking each heifer carefully, then questioned its young owner. Most children talked about feeding schedules and weight gain. Becky's turn came last.

"Her name is Buttercup," Becky began, "and she's got the best pedigree in Arizona. Her registered name is

W.C. Dominetta, number D740529333SVR, out of Dominique, D740529331, and by Battle Prince, number SVR95671402 . . . ." The judge tipped his hat to the back of his head, slipped his thumbs into his jean pockets, trooper style, and smiled.

For the next three minutes, Becky recited the names and dozens of numbers she had so eagerly memorized. When she finished, the judge reached for the microphone. "Six fine heifers, ladies and gentlemen, but my choice for first place is this one." He pointed to Buttercup. "She'll be a strong addition to anyone's herd." Becky had won her blue ribbon.

By the time Bill and I pushed our way through the crowd, a buyer was already running his hand over Buttercup's hips. "Your dad around anywhere, miss?"

"Right here," Bill said. "Glad you like the heifer, but my daughter's the one who can really tell you about her."

As Becky looked at the buyer, tears welled. "She was the best calf we ever had," she began. "But her knees swell up all the time." Her lips trembled now. "She was frozen solid when she was born so she gets sick real easily, and she needs somebody to love her all the time."

"Well now," the buyer said, winking at Bill and me. "How 'bout I take a look at some of those other heifers of yours in the showbarn?"

Bill broke into a knowing smile. "Fine."

On the way home to the ranch, Bill said, "Becky, let's turn Buttercup out to pasture. Exercise might be good for those knees, and with the bloodlines she's got, she'll have one heck of a calf, don't you think?" Becky nodded and hugged her dad.

Four years later, Becky was ready for college. Before she left, we went to the field to admire Buttercup's third calf. "Best calf of the year," Bill said.

Becky grinned. "Daddy, you always did say, 'It's all in the genes.'"

I looked at my husband and then at our daughter. She was still the math whiz, but now she was also a lover of animals and nature. It is in the genes, I thought. They are so alike.

"Hi, Butter," Becky murmured, as we reached the herd. The cow, with her calf at her side, ambled up and lowered her head to be scratched. "She never forgets me, does she?"

I smiled. I knew Becky would never forget her, either, and someday she'd understand that Buttercup had helped her to see what's truly important in life. Through Buttercup, my daughter had learned about the feelings that make us who we are, even if they don't always add up like a nice, neat column of numbers. For Becky, there was now a math of the heart — the math that matters most.

June 11, 1983

I've seen Bill and a visiting rancher drink two pots of coffee in less than an hour. They love the chance to sit and relax. Some visitors stay longer, for lunch, dinner or a week. No matter where they come from it's a long long drive to Singing Valley. But it's the easterners and Californians who puzzle me. After they arrive, the first thing they want to do is trek all the way back to Tucson for boots and jeans so they can "rough it" and "help" Bill. One such visitor is Milton St. John, Bill's cousin Bets' husband.

Milt spent time on a farm growing up. He claimed he had "done it all plenty of times when he was a boy," but today put him to the test. A cow was in trouble, and Bill and Scott had to pull the oversized calf. There was Milt, dressed in new shirt, jeans and boots, dying to help. As Bill wrapped chains around the unborn calf's ankles, I noticed Milt paled a little. Then Scott, who was up to his arm pit inside the cow trying to guide the calf's nose forward said, "Dad. Every time I get a grip on its nose I have to let go to grab the chain to help you and the head turns back. Maybe you better let Uncle Milt take hold of my chain and I'll grip the calf's nostrils and keep it coming forward while you two pull." Milt beamed eagerly. He'd "done this plenty of times — as a boy."

Bill handed him the chain and explained what to do

anyway. "You pull. Then I'll pull . . . see-saw motion. Got it?" Milt nodded courageously, and glanced at Bets who quickly lit another cigarette. The three men worked on that poor calf for five minutes. Finally Scott said, "My arm's numb, Dad, but I've got him straight. Only one more pull. Now!"

The calf shot out, landed on Milt and flattened him. I guess he got the wind knocked out of him because he just lay there, gasping. We told him, "You're a real rancher now, Milt. Two pots of coffee tomorrow, okay?"

THE DUKE OF SINGING VALLEY

It was 6 a.m. when Bill came in for breakfast after morning chores. I was pouring his coffee when the radio announced, ". . . gagged and tied to a chair while her husband plowed the fields, the Cochise County farmer's wife watched helplessly as vandals loaded their furniture into a truck and took off for Mexico."

"That does it," Bill said. "I need to get you a watchdog."

Our cattle and horse ranch had always been a safe place to live. We had never felt a need to take keys out of trucks or tractor ignitions, nor bothered to replace the house keys lost so long ago. But today's radio message was a warning — and it hadn't been the first. When Bill was away, the younger children, Becky and Jaymee, and I needed protection.

The dog had to be trustworthy. Becky and Jaymee were only nine and six. What's more, the dog couldn't harm newborn calves and foals, chase cats or kill chickens. I decided on an English mastiff, a fearsome looking, black-muzzled, gentle giant of a dog, bred for centuries to guard European castles. Surely such a huge animal would be content roaming our alfalfa fields and surrounding rangelands.

Although mastiffs were scarce and expensive, we finally heard of a seven-month-old male. He'd had several previous owners and now another who'd had a change of heart. That should have been a warning.

"He's a little bit — well, timid," said the voice on the line. "I don't have the time or patience to work with him."

"I'll tell you what," the voice purred. "Since I'm leaving on vacation, I'll let you have him for the cost of the crate plus airfare." Another warning I didn't pick up.

At the Tucson airport, a gray fiberglass cage rolled down the cargo conveyor belt upside down. Wadded inside was our eighty-five-pound puppy, wedged on his back. His huge paws were crossed over his chest, corpse-like. The black muzzle waffled against the cage door — his face a mask of misery.

With help, I righted the cage, sank to my knees and reached inside to pat the too-big puppy in the too-small cage. He felt like a loosely stuffed suede beanbag, and beneath the folds of worry cascading down his brow, huge sad eyes fastened on mine. "Now you'll be okay, sweetheart," I murmured. "Let's go home."

When I turned down the last half mile of dirt road to the ranch, I saw Bill waiting, gamely trying to light his pipe in the relentless wind. He's going to love this dog, I thought. It's already as big as a calf, and Bill was a "bigger the better" sort of guy.

I pulled up beside him so he could lift the cage out. "Holy cow," he said, "he weighs more than a bale of hay."

"I've named him The Duke of Singing Valley," I said.

But Bill wasn't listening. Eager to make friends with the watchdog he'd laid out good money for, he crouched on his heels in front of the cage and opened the door. "C'mon, boy," he said. "Get out." The pup shrank back. We tried coaxing him out with hamburger. He screwed his eyes shut. Finally, Bill sat on the ground, placed his boots against the cage frame, grabbed both paws and pulled. The puppy shot out and landed on top of him.

"Good Dukie," I crooned, gripping his collar so I could lead him to the house. It was 105 degrees and the sun was brutal. "Get up now! Let's go." But the terrified pup rolled onto his back and wouldn't budge.

"Let's leave him alone and see what happens," Bill said. Annoyed and disappointed, he mopped his brow and headed toward the barn. "I've got hay to bale," he muttered.

Discouraged, I walked toward the house wondering

what I should do. Suddenly, I felt a snuffling at my heels. I glanced around. Shivering like Jell-O in skin five sizes too large, his tail clamped between his legs, my future "watchdog" lumbered in my shadow.

Our cement porch, shaded with giant pyracantha bushes and sumac, became Duke's home. Rattlesnakes that occasionally coiled on the doormat stayed away now. Barn cats came instead, eager to rub their sinewy bodies against his gentle softness. They were his friends. And when winter arrived we often caught him stacking tiny kittens like kindling wood on the doormat, then he would lie down and tuck them under his massive head and neck to keep them warm.

From the beginning, Duke rarely left the porch unless I came out. Then, with ponderous, lion-like grace he followed in my footsteps, marking boundaries he never roamed beyond. From a book, I learned this trait was bred into a mastiff, an instinct to protect everything inside its territory — to the death, should the need arise.

The children adored him. They rode him bareback and gave him shampoos. They tossed steak bones into his cavernous mouth. Duke thrived and, at two-years-old, weighed 206 pounds and stood three feet tall. Around his neck, a twenty-seven-inch bull chain finally replaced the largest dog collar we could buy.

Meanwhile, robberies and vandalism continued in the valley. A rancher and his wife were murdered while they slept. Could a watchdog have warned them in time? I wondered. Not one like Duke. He was afraid of everything.

Trucks and cars sent him whimpering to me for reassurance. Horses, cows and stray dogs brought him barreling to the front door where he begged to come in.

Chickens scared Duke more than anything else. His first wild howl of terror came one day as he was watching me fill the water cans in the henhouse. I whirled around just in time to catch a hen piercing his leg with her beak. In seconds, provoked by the scent of blood, the entire flock attacked him, screeching, pecking his legs and stabbing at his stomach. Feathers, feed, dust and manure exploded into the air as Duke bolted out the door.

Duke longed to play with calves and foals, but if he ventured too close, the mares and cows terrorized him. On the hottest days he climbed in the cattle tanks. This was partly to keep cool, but also to escape those horns and hooves.

"I think we better get a 'real' watchdog," Bill said one night.

"You mean you're going to get rid of Dukie, Daddy?" Becky's eyes widened.

"We need more protection around here, honey," Bill answered. "I caught a guy stealing hay this morning. If Duke was doing his job, that wouldn't happen."

We kept looking for a sign that Duke wasn't all fear and trembling. Then, at four o'clock one dark morning, Bill and Scott were about to begin baling alfalfa when they heard voices over by the hay barn. Bill jumped into Scott's truck. "Let's go!" Minutes later, in the beam of their headlights, they spotted Duke pacing in front of the wide open barn, whining. Fifteen feet above, on top of the highest bales, seven illegal aliens huddled in terror.

Bill spoke softly to Duke, coaxing him to the house while Scott assured them it was safe to climb down and that his mother would feed them at the picnic table outside.

"Maybe Duke's coming around, Dad," Scott said later. "He really scared the heck out of those guys, didn't he?"

Bill nodded, the first faint flicker of hope in his eyes. "Maybe we won't need another dog after all," he said. But when he went outside after breakfast, there was Duke, wagging his tail, moving from one new amigo to the next, devouring morsels of tortillas. Word travels fast along the border and Singing Valley Ranch would soon become the place where *el buen perro grande* (the nice big dog) lived.

Bill sighed heavily. "I give up."

I was beginning to give up, too, but I didn't want another dog. One was enough, and Duke was my buddy, my friend, somebody to talk to while the girls were in school all day, and Bill out on the ranch. I wasn't alone any more, and gradually I had come to realize that Duke was starting to be protective — in his own special way.

One night, I awoke with a start. Duke was whining. Several weeks earlier, one of our cows that was about to calve had developed a prolapse and had been sewn shut. "Cut the cords as soon as she goes into labor so the calf can get out without tearing her to pieces," the vet had said. Now her calf was due, and we'd been checking her every two hours. Then, dead tired after a long day, I slept through the alarm — finally awakening to Duke's whine.

Quickly, not wanting to wake Bill, I threw on my clothes and dashed with Duke to the corral. The cow lay still, exhausted from straining against the sutures. Two baby hooves had ripped through. I could see the calf's nose and tongue trapped behind them, already blue.

My heart pounded as I cut the surgical strings and

slapped the cow on the side, hard. "Wake up, Mama!" I cried. "Push!" The huge bull calf burst into the world, and Duke bounded around like a hero.

"If it hadn't been for Duke whining, we'd have lost this little one," I told Bill later.

"You're the one who saved it," Bill said, unconvinced.

Duke was always alert, watching for small dangers. When baby cottontails fell into the pool, his frantic whimpering brought us running with a net before they drowned. When a kitten nearly hanged itself in the fork of a tree, Duke sat beneath it and moaned until Scott rescued it.

And there were big dangers — rattlesnakes. One morning as Bill approached his truck he found Duke pacing. Although he was in a hurry, there was something about Duke's behavior that made him hesitate. Then he heard the whir of the diamondback and reached for the shovel he kept in the rear of the truck. A few minutes later, he laid nine rattles on the kitchen table. "Scared the hell out of me," he said.

"How'd you know it was there?"

"Duke." He wasn't so begrudging this time.

Duke was a protector of sorts — at least against the animal world. But what if he had to face the ultimate test of a true watchdog? A man? A gun?

I was pondering this question when a woman running for county supervisor stopped by. When she climbed from her car, carrying a clipboard, Duke suddenly leapt and hit her hand. She wasn't hurt — but the board, pens and papers flew.

Bill was encouraged. He even hung a sign on the gate: BEWARE OF DOG! Then his hope dissolved when a horse buyer arrived a few days later in a helicopter, plunging Duke into a frenzy of fear. He hid behind the log pile for a week.

The day before the Cochise County Fair, Bill slipped a disk in his back, so the girls and I left him at home to take it easy. He was flat-out on the sofa when a choking sound from the porch forced him to get up. One look at the dead Colorado River toad between Duke's paws told him the dog was in serious trouble.

Duke had sunk his teeth into the three-pound toad, crushing the glands that ooze a deadly poison. He was foaming at the mouth, and all the vets were thirty miles away on hand for livestock emergencies at the fair.

The stock trailer was still hooked up to the truck. Bill

knew he couldn't lift Duke into the trailer, and any sign of a leash would make him roll over in the dust and just lie there, unbudgeable. Bill said a prayer and opened the rear gate. "Come on, boy," he said. The suffering dog seemed to know he was trying to help and climbed in.

Forty minutes later, Bill pulled into the fairgrounds where a vet quickly gave Duke two shots: atropine and penicillin. By this time adults and children alike were clinging to the sides of the trailer, peering through the slats and marveling at Duke's size, but fearful of the sounds and froth bubbling from his nose and mouth.

Soon word spread about the vicious dog at Singing Valley Ranch — and Bill savored Duke's fearsome, if undeserved, reputation. "He attacked the county supervisor," party lines buzzed. "Darn near broke her wrist!" "They never keep him on a leash." And at the cafe, the gossip mill relayed a lurid version of events at the fair. "That dog gets so wild he foams and slobbers like a mad thing! The vet had to give him a tranquilizer before he hurt some kids."

One morning when Duke was ten, I found him resting in a hole he had dug for himself beneath the bird-of-paradise bushes by the porch. At first I thought, well, perhaps it's cooler there. I poured food into his bowl. "Come, Dukie," I called. He raised his brows and tried to roll onto his back. "Come on, you lazy old boy," I urged, suddenly remembering the frightened puppy so many years ago, and Bill's disappointment that he wasn't the snarling watchdog he thought we needed.

When he finally managed to get up, I saw the pain. He leaned against me and tried to lie down. Then, at last, he fell.

Hot tears burned as I knelt beside him and pulled his head onto my lap so he could breathe more easily. A deep, heavy sigh rumbled inside him, and suddenly he looked up at me with a sadness in his eyes that will forever haunt me. Duke was gone.

As I buried my face in his forehead and kissed the deep, wrinkled brow, I realized that Duke never did roam those fields of alfalfa or the surrounding rangelands. He simply stayed by my side, guarding our castle.

Suddenly it didn't matter that he'd never been put to the test of a true watchdog. He'd never had to protect me against a dangerous intruder. Instead, Duke had simply shown us love and devotion, warned us when strangers came and signaled us of hidden dangers. In the end, I figured, that was enough.

One day, three years after Duke's death, I was alone on the ranch — the girls off to college, Bill and Scott at an auction. We had talked about getting a new dog, but since

Duke still wandered into my dreams at night, I wasn't ready.

It was dusk when the unfamiliar car crawled down the dirt road toward me. Always glad for company, I waved, but there was something unsettling about the driver. He didn't wave back.

"Hi," I said. "Can I help you?"

"Maybe." His gaze shifted uneasily around the barnyard, slipping beyond fences, and prying into shadows. Slowly, he pushed the car door open. "You still got that big dog of yours?"

Something cold gripped my heart. Then I saw the handgun on the front seat. "Oh, yes!" I said. "He's here somewhere. He nearly took a guy's leg off last week."

The stranger looked hard at me and shut the door again. "I was sorta needin' a job . . . but maybe this place . . . is a little far to come." He stepped on the gas and was gone.

The dust settled and the afternoon slipped toward evening. As I walked toward the house, I felt a snuffling at my heels.

Duke was still there — protecting me.

October 19, 1985

We are now boarding between 60 and 80 horses, which doesn't include our own three stallions and twenty-two mares.

Today was Future Farmers of America Day at Singing Valley Ranch, a much looked-forward-to adventure for high school FFA kids from three counties: Cochise, Santa Cruz and Pima. Many travelled more than 200 miles. But then, that's the way it is in the country for 4-H, FFA and interschool basketball, football and volleyball games. Kids, and grownups, are used to long days, long bus rides and great distances.

Bill had offered a day-long workshop on judging horses for type and confirmation as well as hand-breeding and artificial insemination. He and Scott gave lectures and demonstrations on methods of keeping the stallion under control and techniques used for personal safety and protection of both the mare and stud.

It was a beautiful cool day, and when evening came and the kids gathered around to shake hands and say thanks before leaving, a young pregnant Appaloosa mare that had been restless all day started pawing the ground in earnest. She snorted and paced, demonstrating all the signs they had heard about during the lectures. Then just as it's supposed to happen, the mare circled and crashed to the ground. In minutes, while nearly 100 kids watched and not a word was spoken, she slowly gave birth to a little black and white filly.

The moment of birth, then the first breath of life, has never ceased to thrill me. But we never dreamed we would share this miracle with 100 teenagers, both boys and girls. Eyes filled. Some wept. Finally Bill cheered the moment. "We do it every year," he said. "Planned the whole thing that way — just for you kids."

GOLIATH'S SECRET LIFE

Bill clung to his hat while we hurried to the house after checking three more newborn calves — all heifers. "I wish we'd get some bull calves," he said. "Just our luck one'll come tonight in this storm."

How true, I thought, shivering in the cold March winds that stampeded tumbleweed across our Arizona Hereford ranch. Every time the barometer fell, cows calved, and calving season was at its peak. This time, however, I knew it wasn't only the weather worrying Bill. It was the danger a cow might try to birth a too-big calf.

Less than a year before, he had purchased a fine young bull with modern bloodlines to improve the quality of our cattle. But introducing a new, unproven sire into a herd can be risky to mother and calf because it's the bull that determines the size of newborns. Ranchers want big bulls, the bigger the better, yet at birth, we like both heifer and bull calves to be small, fifty to seventy pounds. The smaller calf doesn't suffer as much trauma in the birthing process. Therefore, it's on its feet faster and is quicker to nurse.

To Bill's disappointment, however, our new bull died of a heart attack, and calves that he had sired were too big. We'd already lost several, but with round-the-clock monitoring and me taking the midnight shift, Bill and our seventeen-year-old son Scott had saved the rest so far by getting to the cow in time, roping her and pulling the oversized baby out before it suffocated in the birth canal.

This particular night, as I headed toward the calving pasture on my all-terrain motorcycle, the wild bobbing of the headlight propelled me into an eerie world. Ghost shadows popped in and out between fence posts. Sneaky shapes slithered along barbed-wire fences. And silver-trunked mesquite trees, familiar in the daylight, became pulsating alien creatures until, at last, the herd of white-faced pregnant cows welcomed me, their eyes aglow like kitchen lamps on distant farms and ranches.

The cattle watched me, unafraid as I cruised among them. Some were lying down, babies cuddled close to their sides. Others stood bunched for warmth, rumps to the wind, but my grip tightened on the handlebars when I spied one cow standing alone in a far-off corner of the field. In my headlight beam, I saw her nose sweeping the ground, nostrils distended, her back humped and her yellow plastic ear-tag flashing like a distress signal. I circled round her. My heart stopped. The unborn calf's back legs extended from beneath her tail, its oversized hoofs turned skyward. Breech birth!

I raced back to the house and awakened Bill and Scott. "We've got trouble," I said. "Big trouble. A breech. Hurry!"

Moments later, his sheepskin collar up around his ears, Bill climbed into the pickup beside me. "Don't worry," he said, "This cow has always raised fine calves. No problems."

However, a breech is rare, and we both knew that no matter how fast a breech calf is pulled out, it is often already dead. Scott arrived armed with chains, an oxygen tank and vet supplies, dread preludes to what lay ahead for the unborn calf slowly smothering to death.

As we pulled up beside her, the cow stood pop-eyed with fear. "Good ole mama," Bill said softly. He slipped a rope halter over her horns and under her chin. Then he tied her securely to the bumper of the truck. "You're gonna be OK."

Scott wrapped the glistening chains around the calf's cold ankles. "This is gonna be rough, Dad," he said. "Huge calf. Look at the heavy leg bone." He handed one chain to his father and gripped the other himself.

"Ready?"

Bill nodded. "You pull first," he cautioned, "then me. See-saw motion. Don't forget." Slowly, inch by inch, the hocks emerged and, finally, the hips. Now the calf had to come out fast because if the chest wall expanded before its head was out, amniotic fluid could be sucked into the calf's lungs. Sitting on the ground, Bill and Scott each braced a boot against the cow's rump.

"OK!" Bill said. "Pull!" Nothing. "Again!" Nothing. On the third try, the calf flopped out on top of them and lay motionless.

Scott scrambled to his feet. "It's a bull, Dad," he shouted, unwinding the chains. "Geez! Look at the size of him! But he's not breathing."

Quickly, Scott wrapped the slippery back ankles in burlap so he could get a good grip. Then he dug his heels into the ground and swung the lifeless body around and around like an Olympic hammer thrower. The centrifugal force, we hoped, would expel any fluid from the newborn's lungs.

When Scott laid the calf back on the ground, Bill dropped to his knees and pumped its chest. Meanwhile, Scott clamped its mouth and one nostril shut and blew into the other. The calf's rib cage rose and fell. We heard gurgling but still no signs of life.

"But I can feel a heartbeat," Bill said. "C'mon, fella . . . breathe." In desperation he poked a stalk of dry grass up the calf's nose. This was an old cowboy trick that had never worked before, but this time the calf sneezed and gulped for air. "Okay!" Bill called out triumphantly. "Let's get him to the barn. Quick."

Back at the barn, we laid the barely alive calf in a straw-filled stall beneath a heat lamp, strapped an oxygen mask on his face and started an I-V. Scott gave him shots of combiotic and banamine to reduce his swollen tongue, but his breathing remained shallow, eyes unfocused. We'd been through this struggle before. We'd seen pneumonia strike. We'd mourned the deaths of beautiful, perfect calves that never awoke from comas.

I rounded up blankets to help keep him warm and threw hay to the frantic mama outside. By now, she was bawling, ramming and raking her horns against the steel stall door to reach her unconscious baby.

It was dawn before Bill came into the kitchen for coffee. Sleep was out of the question. "Biggest calf we ever had," he said, sinking heavily into his chair. "Around 150 pounds."

"Is he still . . . alive?" I was almost afraid to ask.

"That's about it."

"Do you want me to keep an eye on him while you

guys tattoo and tag those baby heifers?"

"Would you?" Bill nodded. I was glad he spared me the usual lecture: "Now don't get too attached." That was a habit of mine with the young, the sick and the helpless. This time, however, the odds of survival were slim. There was no time for love — just comfort and hope.

After breakfast, our two younger children, seven-year-old Becky and four-year-old Jaymee, came with me to the barn. Jaymee peeked under the mound of blankets. "He's so big!" she exclaimed.

"Yes, and only a baby," I reminded her. "Goliath." If he lives, I thought, that's what we'll name him.

Later that afternoon Becky came into the house, "He's still sleeping, Mama. But we're all making him happy." All? During my midnight patrol, I discovered a wild assortment of stuffed animals encircling the calf in the warm golden straw, and cozied beneath the heat lamp, right over Goliath's heart, slept Dracula, an ugly half-grown stray Manx kitten with an ear torn off and a single fang jutting from his lower jaw like a toothpick. Completely wild and untouchable, he glared at me now through slitted eyes.

I sank to my knees anyway and pillowed the feverish calf's head on my lap. Each breath, I knew, could be his last. I stroked the soft curly places behind his ears, the gently sloping forehead and dry pink nose. Fight, little fella, I pleaded. We're going to need you one day.

I longed to go back to bed, but I knew I couldn't leave him to die alone. Dimly aware of the freezing wind whining through the rafters, I dozed for several hours; then, with an eerie feeling of being watched, I suddenly awakened. Dracula, yellow eyes alert, purred contentedly in the infrared glow. I glanced down at the calf. My hopes quickened. Two enormous brown eyes embedded like chocolates in a white velvet cushion stared into mine. I could almost hear Bill's voice again: "Now don't get too attached."

By morning I'd fed the calf two bottles of colostrum. This was first milk that we kept in the freezer for emergencies. He drank greedily and searched my fingers for more. However, he couldn't yet stand. "C'mon, boy," I urged. "Get up!" But when he tried, he toppled and lay bawling and thrashing in the straw.

Later, Bill and Scott made several futile efforts to get him up. "He's probably just sore from being pulled," Bill said.

Meanwhile, the calf's cries were too much for his mama. She'd hooked her front leg over the stall's half door trying to get to her newborn. Bill looked anxiously at her and then at the calf. "That calf's got to nurse," he said. "Let's splint him."

A half hour later Goliath's legs were wrapped in cotton batting and supported within two sections of plastic irrigation pipe. Soon he wobbled around the corral in pursuit of his mother, nursing relentlessly till her udder hung like an empty glove.

"That cow's never going to have enough milk to satisfy such a big calf," I said.

An anxious smile crossed Bill's face. "We're going to have to bottle-feed him. Do you have time?"

Of course I had time! In my mind Goliath was already the cuddly stuffed toy from my childhood. In my heart, I knew he would grow into the storybook bull Ferdinand, who sat under a cork tree all day smelling flowers.

That Goliath would have to be a good herd-sire to pay his way was the farthest thing from my mind. All I cared about was that this soft, fluffy calf's huge, shining eyes brimmed with pleasure at the sight of me when I brought half-gallon bottles of milk. Also brimming with pleasure was little one-fanged Dracula, who licked away the sticky bubbles spilling down Goliath's chin and didn't stop until every hair on the calf's chest and knees were scrubbed clean and white and his hooves shone lacquer bright.

At first, Goliath accepted the cat's ministrations as though they were meant to be. But soon I noticed that every time Dracula departed in search of a hapless mouse, the calf poked his head through the fence and bawled as if to say, Don't go away, I love you! I wondered: was this the beginning of a strange and unusual friendship between a cat so wild no human hands could touch him, and a bull with a heart that could?

Several weeks later, when it was time to cut the splints from Goliath's legs, his weight was already up to 300 pounds. "Gosh, Dad," Scott marveled, "he's doubled his birthweight already. Do you think he'd win a first in the show ring?"

"Hey! Not so fast," Bill said. "He looks like he'll have the size, but don't forget, it isn't blue ribbons that make a good breeding bull."

Even as Goliath's extraordinary growth continued, Bill saw problems. Clearly our long-legged calf spent far too much time lying down. And when he walked his hips sashayed. "Might help to put him out in a larger pasture," Bill suggested. "He can run with the other calves and get some exercise."

But Goliath promptly chose a shady place by an old windmill and plopped down. It wasn't the cork tree I'd dreamed about, and he wasn't smelling flowers, but he seemed content. Still, I worried, does he hurt?

He didn't seem to mind when his mama took off to graze all day without him. Instead of romping and butting heads as bull calves do, or terrorizing tarantulas and toads with stomping hooves, he seemed content to watch the other calves play. There, beside the windmill, he waited for the feed wagon, rubbed his itchy horn buds against the cement foundation and bobbed his head with pleasure at the sight of Dracula, the ugly cat that still found this quiet calf's soft, warm back a comforting place to be.

Soon Goliath graduated from half-gallon bottles to a pail full of milk. Lugging heavy buckets became a nuisance and Bill decided grain would be just fine. "Make him come and get it," he suggested. "As a matter of fact, don't let him have it right away. You know. Take him for a walk." I could tell Bill thought this was a great idea.

One day he pulled up beside me laughing. "All you need's a flute," he said. "You look just like the Pied Piper."

I knew what he meant. Behind me lurched Goliath; Dracula followed at his heels so he could snarl at the five or six curious barn cats that tagged along, our mastiff, Duke, one overweight dachshund, Daisy, and a few assorted chickens bringing up the rear.

The children and I visited Goliath often. Unlike other calves that ran away if we came too close, this one didn't. His dark eyes shone expectantly. "He knows we're bringing Oreos," Jaymee said, skipping alongside. Goliath loved chocolate, and the girls squealed with laughter when he licked the treat from their palms with his sandpaper tongue, chewed for several minutes, then probed each of his nostrils with the tip, savoring the lingering aroma.

At weaning Goliath weighed 800 pounds, by far the heaviest and largest of all our bull calves that year, but he still sashayed.

"I'm afraid we better steer him," Bill said one night, meaning Goliath should be castrated. "He'll make a great

4-H project for a kid to feed, show and sell."

"Oh, Daddy!" Becky cried out. "Then he'll be auctioned for meat!"

"He's too good to steer," I said.

"Good for what?" Bill asked. "Odds are that a bull his size with a weakness in the hindquarters won't be able to mount a cow to breed her. Also, he might be sterile from the high temperature he ran at birth."

"We don't know that for sure," I argued. "He's only ten months old. Give him a little more time."

Eight weeks later, Goliath was so scared of the scales he almost fell down when we tried to shove him onto the wobbly platform. I couldn't bear the thought of Bill or Scott clipping a ring in his nose. He didn't need one like the other bulls.

"Goliath's too gentle for that treatment," I said, putting my arms around his neck. I tugged a little. "C'mon, sweetheart," I coaxed, "get on with me." Together we weighed 1140 pounds — that meant my beautiful bull weighed 1001! A record for us.

As a reward for Goliath's bravery, I grabbed Dracula, one of the few times I ever managed to touch him, and set him on the bull's back. The cat, who hadn't attached himself to anything, human or beast, until Goliath came along, relaxed instantly on the bull he'd grown to love, and I led my Ferdinand around the barnyard — ringless — on a simple rope halter.

Scott groaned. "You're making a real sissy out of that bull, Mom," he said. But I didn't care. Why didn't anyone understand that Goliath was just a little different from ordinary bulls?

Bill had other thoughts. "He'll weigh over 2000 pounds in another year. That's over a ton of hay a month, plus feed, vaccinations, worming. Thousands of dollars! That's an awful expense for a bull that may or may not be able to breed." In other words, Goliath had to go.

"But you need a bull with his bloodlines," I countered. "A new bull's expensive too! Isn't it worth the try?"

Bill looked thoughtful. "I'm going to start an artificial insemination program," he said. "It's the cheapest way to introduce a new bloodline, and safer than buying a new unproven bull. Scott and I have already selected thirty good cows and heifers."

"That's a great idea," I said. "Then you can give Goliath a chance. Put him out in the pasture a month after you've inseminated the last one. If any come back in heat, he can breed them, and when calves arrive a month late, we'll know they're his. He'll have a chance to prove himself."

Smoke curled from Bill's pipe. "Okay, we'll give it a try," he said. I knew it might not be what he preferred, but still, it was also tough for him to throw away the biggest bull we'd ever had. That fall, Bill enrolled Scott and himself in the A-I (artificial insemination) course offered by Arizona State University in Phoenix.

Then winter closed in. While our older herd-sires were removed from their pastures and brought into separate corrals to rest and regain valuable weight lost in the line of duty, Goliath, too, was confined to a large corral where, unlike every bull we'd ever had, his affection for other barnyard animals showed. He let chickens peck away lice from his ears and flies from his ankles. Rattleheaded doves shared his grain. Cactus wrens nested in his hay bin, and when he slept with his chin on the ground, Dracula crouched nearby waiting to pounce on invisible mice stirred up by Goliath's nostrils puffing in the dust.

By April 30 the following spring, Bill and Scott had finished artificially breeding thirty cows. On May 31, with doubt in his heart, Bill turned Goliath loose in the windmill pasture.

The huge bull fixed his dark eyes on his future and snorted loudly. Gone was my oversized pet with the tranquil disposition.

Now, lowering his rack of grappling horns, 2000 pounds of muscle and brawn pawed the ground, then sashayed into the midst of a wide-eyed herd and announced his intent in a deep, rich baritone.

Towering over the cows, his upper lip curled back over his nostrils exposing a roguish smile, Goliath represented the epitome of raw masculinity. But like most inexperienced young bulls, he spent his entire first day making a nuisance of himself chasing and beseeching heifers who wanted nothing to do with him because they weren't in heat. This is the only time a cow will submit to a bull, and Goliath, a novice at the game, didn't know the difference.

Then the second day I saw a fetching two-year-old

heifer rouse his passion to uncontrollable heights. Wheezing and sweating, he lumbered after her, rolling up more miles in a single afternoon than he'd covered in his entire life. All through the ordeal Dracula followed, boxing the foot-long tuft on the end of Goliath's tail or clinging to it with his claws and swinging, making it doubly difficult for the bull to woo his beloved.

By nightfall Goliath's voice was a croak and his front legs and chest were swollen and bleeding from the vicious kicks bestowed by his intended. She simply wasn't ready.

The following morning we found Goliath with his chin on the ground. The object of his desire batted her two-inch eyelashes at him six feet away. Imagining I saw despair in the bull's eyes, I asked Bill, "Could he die from frustration?"

"No. But she probably crippled him for good," was the gloomy response. "Let's hope he learned a lesson."

Later that day we installed a bull feeder in the pasture, a metal trough in a cage large enough for only one animal at a time. Perhaps food is the best antidote for a broken heart, I thought, happy to see Goliath struggle to his feet as high-powered pellets clattered into the trough. Before

Goliath could get to the feeder, however, the heifer that had spurned his affections moved toward the cage.

Limping both front and back now, he booted her away and buried his head in the trough. What's more, it didn't take long for the rest of the herd to learn this feeder — now his feeder — was off-limits. If he couldn't breed them, Goliath seemed to be saying, at least he would demand their respect.

Meanwhile, Bill's hopes for his artificial-insemination program were soaring. Since a cow's gestation period is nine months, it would be six more months before we saw results of the A-I effort — and eight before we'd know if Goliath had sired any calves.

One moonless June night, less than three weeks after we put Goliath in the windmill pasture, Bill and I were about to go to bed when angry bellowing knifed the darkness. "Bull fight!" Bill said, grabbing his hat. "I'll bet Herman broke out again!"

Herman was an aging, ill-tempered 2000-pound Hereford bull from a ranch less than a mile away. He'd been content on his forty-acre field with the same three cows for quite some time, but as far as a bull is concerned, breeding season is all year long should the opportunity arise. Friends had told us earlier that neither barbed wire nor metal gates could stop Herman once he got the urge.

"I'm taking the jeep," Bill said. "You better follow me in the pickup."

My scalp tightened. "Why?"

"I'm no matador," he muttered.

I followed, my hands sticking to the steering wheel as the land rolled by like silent film in shades of black and gray. Suddenly, Bill stopped short. Across the road in front of him lay thirty-five feet of fence posts and five-strand barbed wire. Beyond the tangled mass two huge bulls roared, eyes ablaze, white faces glowing like skulls in the night.

Bill had told me that a bull will take on any number of other bulls at one time when there is a danger of losing his mate. He will fight to the death if need be. That's why we kept our bulls in separate pastures with their own herds. But what about Goliath? He was such a gentle bull. Had a one-night fling with a teasing heifer been enough to stir the mighty protectiveness lying dormant inside him?

My heart pounded as Bill climbed from the jeep, gripping a five-foot two-by-four. Now as he approached the two huge bulls, their horns crashed together and sparks lit up the night like fireworks.

What if Bill gets hurt? My breath caught. What if Goliath gets killed? Clouds of dust muted the scene. With his board, Bill whacked the two raging bulls on their heads, then on the back. He might as well have used a feather. Angry, helpless, he jumped back into the jeep and drove the vehicle straight into them.

When the dust settled, a strange tableau came into focus: Herman, looking ambushed and defeated, was skulking home; and Goliath, soaked with blood, was basking in the affections of his adoring cows as they licked the wounds on his face, neck and shoulders. As for Bill, he was leaning against the jeep puzzling over how to keep thirty cows and a bull in a field for the rest of the night with the fence torn down. "Well, if Goliath can't do anything else," he said, grinning, "at least he knows how to fight."

With August heat came torrential rain, flies and the need to worm and vaccinate all the cattle on our ranch against disease. It was late afternoon and about to pour again as we funneled Goliath, who now weighed 2300 pounds, and his cows single file into the thirty-foot-long, four-foot-wide metal-railed chute, to give them the necessary injections. All thirty-one animals, knee deep in mud, were wedged in head to tail, and Goliath rested his chin on the cow's hips in front of him.

"This bunch is a heck of a lot easier to work on than those other crazy cows today," Scott commented.

"They have a real leader," I said. "There's no reason for them to fidget. Goliath's so big and quiet he's like a king-sized security blanket."

Then, just as Scott anchored himself to the top rail to give the next animal in line its shots, the cows suddenly started bawling, falling and trying to climb out. Scott was thrown on his back to the ground. He struggled to his feet, his face white with panic. "Dad! They're being electrocuted!" he screamed. A 250-volt buried cable had grounded itself against one of the metal panels, charging them all. Because of his massive size, Goliath couldn't move. Neck arched, walleyed with fear and pain, he opened his mouth and bellowed.

Bill ran to the main circuit box and threw the breaker switch. Cattle whimpered and fell. Those already on the ground strained to get up while Scott hurried for crowbars to open the chute where all lay alive but hopelessly trapped. As he and Bill worked to free the terrified animals, those closest to Goliath rested their heads against his sides seeking comfort. My Ferdinand lends an aura of calm in a time of terror, I thought.

Winter slipped into spring. The artificially inseminated cows began to calve. With each birth, Bill and Scott tried to recall which of the two had handled the specific insemination. At the month's end, the score was seven to six. Scott won. The calving ceased. "Damn," Bill said. "Only thirteen out of thirty."

"How come so few?" I asked.

"We're just beginners," said Scott, shrugging his broad shoulders. "Like anything else, it takes practice."

"Maybe we didn't do such a good job," Bill suggested.

"We should have put a good bull in the pasture with them, Dad. Now we've got seventeen unbred cows."

"You're forgetting Goliath," I said, unwilling to give up hope.

"Goliath who?" Scott asked with a grin.

"Oh, come on. Trust me."

Thirty days after the last calf from artificial insemination was born, Goliath's first passion produced twin bulls. Sixteen more healthy calves followed, all fathered by Goliath. Not one was too big at birth, and nearly all had the traits Bill had hoped for: long legs, stocky builds and calm dispositions. Still the question gnawed: With bad legs and problems of weight and mounting, how'd Goliath do it?

And then I knew the answer. Goliath wasn't just bigger, he was smarter. Unlike other bulls, he discovered the chase wasn't necessary. He knew his limitations and he learned that patience was the secret. All he had to do was curl his upper lip back over his nostrils into a smile, and his loves would come to him at his favorite place beside the windmill. When the right moment came, he'd

get the job done.

Over the years there came a gradual change to our ranch. Irrigation transformed parched lands into lush, green fields, and uniform herds of bigger-bodied, longer-legged cattle replaced the cows of the past. Only one thing remained the same: An old bull, surrounded by calves, rested by the windmill just as he had in his youth. Birds perched on his spectacular horns, singing their hearts out in spite of the cat with one fang curled atop his mahogany hide.

I wished time could go on forever, but, of course, it couldn't — not for us, and especially not for Goliath. The afternoon came when my hand tightened on his last bucket of feed laced with the daily dose of bute to ease the pain. I knew we had to put Goliath down.

He didn't seem to know I was there till I knelt beside him to bestow the usual loving hug. When he opened his chocolate eyes, the chill wind of a cold March night drifted up through the years to me. In my memory I saw a newborn calf struggling to live and once more I heard my wish: "We're going to need you one day." Now — on his last day — I scratched the curly places behind his ears, right where he loved it most, and murmured farewell to the best bull we ever had, my Ferdinand.

We buried Goliath in our cattle graveyard beyond the

White River draw. There were many mounds there now. But that first day, and others after that, I saw Dracula, an old wildcat with one fang, cozied up on top of the biggest mound — right where the heart should be. He was mourning the biggest and best friend he ever had. We did too.

The Rest of the Story

THE REST OF THE STORY

Our four older children, Emmy, Bud, Jennifer and Scott, agree the move was hard for them at the time. Today they feel it was the best thing that ever happened because for the first time in their lives they had to struggle. Suddenly life wasn't all fun and games.

At the same time they grew closer, for all they had was each other. Old friends lived three thousand miles away. Trips to Tucson were a four-hour round trip. Every telephone call was long distance and costly, so limits had to be set. Add to that a four-party line — they soon discovered that talking for hours on the phone was impossible.

Our TV on the ranch often had only one clear channel. More often it didn't work at all. It wasn't long before the kids were reading more, and talking with one another far more than they had done in the past. Because of this, and the reality of practically no social activities, they rediscovered their sisters and brothers, and gradually the boys came to know and work with their dad. Then school started, high school, and being so close to the Mexican border a whole new culture opened up to them.

Becky and Jaymee were westerners from the start. Rural schools, 4-H, FFA, animals and nature were their world. The only TV program worth watching was "Little House on the Prairie." They never missed an episode. A few months ago Jaymee ordered the whole set and is watching them all over again with her husband, David Hernandez.

Today, all six of our children are leading busy, productive lives.

Emmy and Mike Baker both work for United Technologies in Hartford, Connecticut. Mike is Chief Pilot and Emmy is Flight Attendant Supervisor and flies all over the world countless times a year.

Bud and his wife, Kathy, live in Colorado Springs where he is a Facilities Engineer at Falcon Air Force Base and Kathy is a homemaker. Bud worked on the ranch for years. Today he and his dad are in close touch via e-mail and telephone. We don't see enough of him, and plan a trip to Colorado next summer.

Jennifer is retired after fifteen years of teaching high school children with learning disabilities. She and her husband, Manny Molina, have three teenage children; Matthew, Michelle and Michael. Jennifer is president of

Experience Atlanta, a destination management company she coordinates from her home in Atlanta, Georgia. They are planning a move back to Phoenix, Arizona as I write.

Scott, who worked on the ranch with us for fifteen years, and his wife, Dian, have three children; William, Jonathan and Meghan. Scott now works for the Pima County Department of Environmental Quality in the Household Hazardous Waste Department of Tucson.

Becky and her husband, Mel Council, Technical Writer for West Air, live in Fresno, California. Becky is the Controller for Horizon High Reach.

After eight years of marriage, Jaymee is enjoying being the mother of her babies, Nicholas and Alex. She and her husband, David Hernandez, President of H & K Waste Management Company have built a log cabin in the Cochise Stronghold. Jaymee works for David's company but does it from home. "Maybe I'm old-fashioned," she says, "but our children need me. So does David. Besides, I'm proud to be 'just a housewife' after working in a bank for seven years. Now I'm a mommy. That's far more important."

Bill is retired now. Health problems caught up and he had to give up ranching and move to Tucson. He is active in a local group of Ex-Prisoners of War and served recently as Commander of the Cochise County Chapter of Ex-POWs. He attends meetings every Monday night at the Veteran's Hospital where he and fellow ex-prisoners of war share their life stories and "sure-fire" solutions to America's problems.

And me? I like to let the years pass gently through my mind for I have come to love this prickly, thorny, twisted land where the sun turns love-grass gold. Rooted in my memory are the gentle sounds of the desert: the rustle of lizards and quail in the brush; the laughter of my children playing tag with the tumbleweed; the distant rumble of cattle trucks rolling down dusty roads, and the cry of an abandoned calf in the night or the eerie song of the coyote.

I remember the wind: pleasant and wistful on some days, but on others so severe it wrenched limbs from trees, peeled back roofs from barns, and created terrifying dust storms that sand-blasted paint from houses, tractors and brand new vehicles.

But mostly, I remember waiting for rain — a desert celebration when it came: rivers of water restoring life and color to the arid lands and the searing, smog-filled sky; flowers and frogs, clean air, and when it was all over, a red-tail hawk gliding across a fiery sunset. That's when I like to write at my desk, where gold dust hangs in shafts of sunlight filtering through my kitchen windows.

How lucky I am to have lived two different lives with the same man. I wish for the sake of children that everyone could. There is no time for loneliness when you care and share. Not too long ago a young, single mom asked me, "How could you stand having to feed him three times a day and doing nothing on Saturday nights but the dishes?" I wanted to answer but a strange sense of guilt stopped me, a need to cover up the fact that dumb and out of vogue as it might sound today, I love being with him. We didn't need costly entertainment. We are best friends. We are close to our children, maybe not geographically but in heart. We talk and listen to each other, and make a few sacrifices. That's the secret.

A short time after the young mom asked me these questions, a long distance phone call came from a girl friend of college days. Of course I asked right away, "How's John?"

"Well, I'm finally in step with the times," she trilled. "It took me forty-six years but I finally got rid of him and I'm on my way to the Caribbean."

Forty-six years? . . . in step with the times? I was stunned. I do not agree with the social mores of the late twentieth-century America. Marriage is for keeps. Besides, I love my husband. I wouldn't care if he turned purple. Living, talking with and loving the same man is like riding a roller coaster. You share the ride together — all the ups and downs — and focus on the bright side. It's the biggest thrill of your life if you want it to be. All you have to do is hang on tight so nothing falls apart.

Not too long ago Bill and I were reminiscing about the ranch when suddenly I remembered my romantic dreams of thirty years ago — "the west" — and what I thought it would be. Softly, I said, "Hey," and looked him straight in the eye. "How come we never had any campfires, and steak and beans, and someone to strum a guitar?"

His blue eyes sparkled mischievously, and his cheeks bunched into that same irresistible grin of more than fifty years ago. "That stuff's fiction," he said. "Besides, we never had the time."

And we laughed together.